Florence

LOVE'S GREATEST MISTAKE

LOVE'S GREATEST MISTAKE

BY

FREDERIC ARNOLD KUMMER

ILLUSTRATED WITH SCENES
FROM THE PHOTOPLAY
A PARAMOUNT PICTURE

NEW YORK
GROSSET & DUNLAP
PUBLISHERS

Made in the United States of America

Copyright, 1927, by
LIBERTY WEEKLY, Incorporated

Copyright, 1927, by
GROSSET & DUNLAP

LOVE'S GREATEST MISTAKE

CHAPTER I

It was Don Kendall who invited Honey to the Troup housewarming—invited her, and took her in his glittering roadster. Don himself was inclined to glitter at times, but Honey rather liked the polish that caused it.

There had been a warm and very persuasive note in his voice as he whispered the invitation over the telephone.

"Doing anything tonight?" he had asked. "Hope not, because Ben Troup's just opening his new shack on Beechwood Avenue. Throwing a whale of a party. Not a bad scout, Ben, even if he is hard pan. Real, anyway. If you need a chaperon, why not bring that good-looking sister of yours? Ben will like her, if she's nice to him. He's reached the grateful age. Don't miss this, Honey. It'll be *some* party. Ben says joy is going to be so unrefined that even the china doorknobs will blush.

You're game, aren't you? I'll take good care of you. How about it?"

"I—guess so," Honey said slowly.

She had never been to such a party, and the idea rather frightened her. Then she remembered the slogan of her girl friends—" Be a good sport or send for the undertaker "—and assumed a not overconfident gayety. "Of course I'd like to go—a lot!"

"Fine. I'll stop around for you about eight-thirty. Pick up your sister on the way back, if she decides to go. And if her husband's in town we'll take him too. The more the merrier! Wear your light running togs, darlin'. There's going to be some stepping out. 'By."

Honey sat at the cheap wooden table that held the telephone instrument, wrapped in a mantle of dreams. A picture of Don Kendall came between her eyes and the gay drift of sunlight through the hall window. Very tall and big he was, and handsome as an athlete is handsome. The mere thought of him gave her astonishing thrills. "The face of an angel and the morals of a tom-cat," some town gossip had once described him.

Instead of an angel, Honey preferred to picture him as a blond viking, mailed, steel-capped, tremendous, driving his ship over the cold Norse seas to berserk victory. There were reasons, of course, for this. Dreams are variously pieced: some distantly remembered romance, read in childhood; or the fact that Don's father was president of a great steamship company, or that the young man himself had ridden the high air in France to joyous combat over the trenches.

No; Honey did not think of angels when she thought of Don, although she did wonder at the tenderness that brought him so often to their small Pennsylvania town to see his grandmother. Mrs. Donald Kendall, at seventy, was herself a gay warrior, battling valiantly against the invincible army of age. The two, no doubt, had much in common.

As for Don's morals, Honey knew he had his reputation; but to be one of "the" Kendalls in that small town excused most things. Even as a child, Honey had realized that Don and his friends, home from college, could steal barber poles or remove the bronze ladies from the courthouse fountain without serious consequences, while had her sober brother, Martin, attempted anything of the sort, he would doubtless have cooled his heels for sixty days in jail.

4 LOVE'S GREATEST MISTAKE

Don could even drive his car down Main Street at express-train speed and the traffic policeman smiled pleasantly and looked the other way.

It meant something to be the only son of Matt Kendall, who lived in New York and owned a steamship line.

Honey's father, "Pop" McNeill, owned nothing to speak of—not even the house he lived in, although he worked hard enough for the "party" and held a position of some importance in the Department of Public Works. The gulf, social and financial, between Honey McNeill and Don Kendall had grown wider very rapidly indeed since he had taken up his residence in New York.

She had seen little of him in the last few years. The pride of the Kendall family spent most of his time in New York, where opportunity to spend money joyously was greater and the night's thousand eyes conveniently winked. During his occasional visits to the big stone house in Greene Avenue, where his grandmother lived in solitary grandeur, he had often met Honey on the street and talked to her.

What, Honey wondered, was the reason for his sudden interest in her since his arrival in town some two weeks before? She had once heard her older and rather cynical married sister, Jane Sommers, say that men frequently married women because they could not get them in any other way. Why, Honey thought, should she not make Don care for her that much? She must look her best for him at Mr. Troup's party. And, since her own wardrobe had very narrow limitations, she decided to seek help from Jane.

She found her sister in the little tile-and-stucco bungalow on Oak Avenue which was George Sommers' nearest approach to a castle in Spain. Jane was in the kitchen, peeling potatoes. In her blue cotton-crêpe wrapper and towel-tied head, she did not much resemble the glorious young person whom George had led to the altar some five years before. Yet, by the use of facial creams and massage, vigorous exercise, the simple foods of semipoverty, and the refusal to bear children, Jane had succeeded in keeping her good looks almost intact.

Honey was often puzzled because she went to such pains in the matter. Certainly it was not to please her husband. Poor, plodding, unimaginative George always thought her

6 LOVE'S GREATEST MISTAKE

perfect, even in a cotton wrapper. Perhaps, far back in her mind, Jane nursed a hazy hope that some day, somehow, she would gain through her good looks all the lovely and expensive things her heart desired.

Honey understood and could sympathize with her sister's basic discontent. Jane's marriage had not turned out as Honey hoped her own would.

Thoughts of Don suddenly filled Honey's imagination. How glorious it would be to spend their honeymoon in Hawaii! And then they would tour the Orient, perhaps the world. When they returned they would live, of course, in New York—except for a few weeks in winter when they would go to Florida, and the heat of summer would find them in either Newport or Maine.

She would have her own motor—a small sedan, as dainty and swift as a fawn—and quite frequently—possibly as often as two or three times a week—she would arise early and drive Don to his office. There would be no housework to worry about; she could have all the servants she wished.

Housework! Honey's thoughts returned quickly to the towel-tied head and wrapper-

LOVE'S GREATEST MISTAKE

enfolded figure of Jane. With a surge of pity she remembered that Jane had dreamed of winters in Florida and summers in Maine and a motor of her own. Would Honey's dreams ever come true? Would Jane's?

The cruelly clear insight of youth made Honey doubt Jack's chances, and the shadow of the same thought overcast her own bright visions. Did marriage always end in disappointment?

Of course George might become rich; but as a plodding drummer selling electric washing-machines this seemed unlikely—as unlikely as that the beautiful wings of a butterfly would suddenly sprout from her own lovely back.

There was the possibility of a second husband, of course, but that would involve getting rid of George—something to which, Honey felt sure, Jane had not, so far, given consideration. She had just drifted along, sewing, scrubbing, peeling potatoes, waiting for George to come home from his continual trips.

Dull; unexciting; almost unendurable at times.

There were other ways besides marriage, Honey knew, whereby a woman of beauty might obtain wealth in return for—well, in return for being beautiful. Such ways Jane had not considered. Honey knew. Not definitely. Her thoughts seemed blurred. She drifted, determined to keep her good looks against some possible future glowing romance in which George had no part. So many married women—young married women without children—dream such dreams.

Honey entered her sister's kitchen as gay and bright as the morning sunshine that came in with her.

"Hello, sis," she said. "How's everything?"

"All right." Jane began to take off her rubber gloves. "Same old grind. George is in Scranton. Home Saturday. What's new? You look all pepped up."

Honey lighted a cigarette. She did not particularly care for cigarettes, but they seemed to go with certain moods and occasions.

"Ben Troup, the contractor, is giving a big party tonight," she said. "Don Kendall has asked me to go. I can take you if I like. So I thought if you would lend me that green chiffon dress of yours—the one with the rhinestone shoulder straps—"

"But we don't know Mr. Troup," Jane

objected, regarding her sister with a cool and reflective eye.

"Father does—they went to school together. And, anyway, it's Mr. Kendall who's asking us."

Again Jane Sommers stared.

"Don Kendall doesn't give a rap whether I go or not," she said. "Why this sudden interest in *you?*"

"I don't know. The point is, do we go to the party or don't we? I can't go without you. I'll have to spend the night here. The family would raise the roof if I didn't get home by twelve. Come on, Jane. You'll enjoy it. George Sommers doesn't expect you to sit at home crocheting foot warmers while he's on the road, does he? Let me try on that chiffon, anyway. You could wear your black georgette. It shows off your figure beautifully."

"All right."

Jane began to unwind the towel from her long and really beautiful hair.

The appeal of romance had reached her. Why should life be lived in such uninteresting grooves, when the Great Adventure might be just around the corner? It was sweet, unutterably sweet, to be pursued, desired. When

George came home from his eternal trips, he demanded a huge meal, said he was worn out from riding on trains, went to sleep very early, snoring.

Was that all of life?

"This green just suits me," Honey laughed, executing a gay Charleston. "I'll be a knockout, sis. Wouldn't this old burg throw a fit if I married Don Kendall?"

"Swell chance!" Jane mumbled, her mouth full of pins.

CHAPTER II

Don Kendall drove away from the Mc-Neill's old house on Grove Street with a hard and reckless hand upon the wheel. A man to take chances, Honey thought. She rather liked that. When he leaned over and told her how lovely she was, she breathed a contented sigh.

After they had stopped for Jane, the small seat was so pleasantly crowded that Honey could feel the warm pressure of Don's shoulders against her own. It made her heart quicken. Had she fallen in love with him in the past two weeks? She looked at his ruddy, daring face and concluded that she had— almost.

At the Troup house, ablaze with lights, they were promptly hurried to the cellar. A huge, dimly lit cavern, it seemed to Honey, as they descended the steps. A crowd was milling about, laughing, talking. Blue-gray smoke from cigars and cigarettes rolled in billows about their heads. Red lanterns, hanging from the rafters, smoldered through the tobacco smoke, giving the suggestion of fire.

A real, old-fashioned bar with a brass foot rail had been set up along the wall, with two Negro bartenders, like ebony marionettes, eternally mixing, pouring. Liquor in a continual flood—pre-war liquor, somebody said. Ben Troup was the sort to look ahead, to provide against future aridness.

"Just like old times," Don laughed, his arm around Honey's slim shoulders, his foot on the brass rail. "Have another, Beautiful? It won't hurt you. Gasoline has ruined more young girls than alcohol."

Amid much laughter Honey heard over her shoulder the last words of a story that would have chilled her had she understood it.

Pictures crowded Honey's brain. Amazing pictures. Bits torn from a mad dream. A girl, the shoulder straps of her evening gown broken, danced a Charleston on a table top while a circle of men applauded.

Everywhere were couples in dark corners. The place reeked of sex—like a perfume deadly, intoxicating. Was it that, Honey wondered, which made such parties alluring? Occasional curses, scraps of vulgarity, smacked of low

LOVE'S GREATEST MISTAKE

dance halls. The music suggested the thick, torrid atmosphere of the jungle. Yet Honey felt the fascination of the bizarre.

The vivid, sentient atmosphere of the place, the reek of alcohol, tobacco, perfume, the odors of human flesh, the primitive, urging music, all went to Honey's head like some violent and dangerous wine. She moved through it, her pulses throbbing staccato in the soft round column of her throat. Drumming jungle melodies sounded in her ears. Nothing theretofore had affected her so vividly.

Ben Troup had risen from the mud—had begun his career as a contractor by wielding a shovel at a concrete mixing trough. His friends and acquaintances ranged from the crooked politicians of the City Hall crowd, and the Chief of Police, up through bootleggers, dealers in contractors' supplies, to the vice-president of a local bank in which Ben's money had made him a director.

The party, called by courtesy a housewarming, celebrated in fact the granting of Mr. Troup's recent divorce. The illiterate gray-haired wife of his pick-and-shovel days had been dumped cruelly but quite legally upon the scrap heap, to make room for a younger and more attractive mate.

Halfway through the evening, Honey had a brief conversation with her sister. It took place in one of the dressing-rooms set apart for the women, where Mrs. Sommers was trying to mend a rip in her black georgette dress.

"Look out for that Kendall boy, Honey," Jane said. "Ten minutes alone with him would ruin any woman's reputation."

Honey lifted her delicate but rather determined chin.

"I can take care of Don Kendall, sis," she said.

"I know." Jane let her voice express her skepticism. "But it's you I'm thinking about. Can you take care of *yourself?* Watch your step."

Don, when Honey rejoined him, walked toward the steps.

"What do you say if we take a look over the house?" he laughed. "It's as full of rooms as a Swiss cheese is of holes."

In the main hall he took Honey by the arm, guided her toward the staircase.

They went up slowly, stepping around several couples. From the voices that floated down to them, Honey knew that there were many more guests on the floor above. The large upstairs sitting-room held a dozen at least, gathered round a bottle-covered table.

Don stopped for a moment in the doorway, saw a woman start toward him, turned back.

"No room for us in there," he laughed. "What's this ahead of us?" He pushed open the door of a small, dimly lit room, and stepped inside. "Ben's private study, I suppose."

Beneath shaded amber lights Honey caught a glimpse of Chinese rugs, an inlaid Moorish desk, low chairs, a couch heaped with cushions, green, orange, black. For a man's study, the effect was curious, to say the least. It was equally odd that such a man as Ben Troup should have a study at all.

Honey turned to go out. The door had swung almost shut. Not quite, however. The air suddenly became charged with possibilities. Panic seized upon Honey. She wanted to escape. Yet her legs refused to carry her. They trembled a little.

Then, without warning, Don Kendall swept her into his arms, bent to kiss her.

Held crushed and helpless, Honey fought

16 LOVE'S GREATEST MISTAKE

desperately to retain her grip on the world of solid things. But it came to her in a flash of fear that if Don bent her back a very little farther, smothered her senses a little longer beneath that blinding kiss, she would be lost utterly—to no real purpose that she could quite understand.

Her hands were like ice, her cheeks burning, as cold reasoning and the hot blood of youth sought equally to possess her. With fingers that struggled blindly to force Don's face away, she found herself caressing him—and hating herself for it.

Her effort to scream resulted in no more than a feeble gasp. She heard an inner voice whispering cruelly, "You have wanted to know about life—this *is* life."

Don was hurting her lips, bruising them, crushing her against his chest.

"Please—Don—let me go!" she gasped.

But he drew her still closer.

"I want you—love you!" he whispered.

For a delicious, terrifying moment Honey believed him. Then she looked into his eyes —saw there, not love, but something fierce, savage, cruel—and her weakness left her.

"Let me alone, Don!" she cried, tearing

herself swiftly from his grasp. "Don't touch me!"

The man gave her a quick, wide stare, then dropped his arms to his sides.

"All right," he said, and, wheeling, jerked open the door. In the hall outside stood Jane and a slender, rather studious-looking young man whose eyes seemed abnormally big behind shell-rimmed glasses.

"I've been looking for you everywhere," Jane said, with a swift glance at Honey's flushed face. "Meet Mr. Gibbs."

Honey put out her hand, introduced the two men.

"Don Kendall has been showing me over the house," she laughed, with a little note of self-consciousness.

Don, in the doorway behind her, was lighting a cigarette.

"May I have a dance?" Gibbs asked.

"Why—certainly." Honey placed her hand on his arm.

As she turned away she felt Don's gaze upon her—hard, questioning. Suddenly it came to her that she might never see him again. A terrifying thought!

CHAPTER III

Honey opened her eyes, stretched her arms high above her head, and yawned. One of the green holland shades had not been drawn quite down. By the light that filtered through, she saw that the clock on Jane's dresser marked half-past ten.

Her sister, in the other twin bed, was still sleeping soundly, without any of the aids to beauty she usually put on before retiring. When she had come in, Honey did not know. She herself had been brought home by Herbert Gibbs at half-past three.

The party had become rather "thick" by that time and Honey had had enough of it. So had Mr. Gibbs. He lived in New York, it seemed, and was connected with the firm of architects that had designed the new local City Hall. His reasons for going to Mr. Troup's party had been business ones.

Sitting up in bed, Honey tried to crystallize her impressions of the previous evening. She and Gibbs had danced together a number of times. She had found him a good but not an inspired dancer. Don Kendall moved with a panther's grace.

It had not pleased her that Jane had monopolized Don for the remainder of the evening, even though she had found Mr. Gibbs a pleasant companion. He *had* talked a little too much about his work, Honey thought; but he was nice.

As for Don Kendall—she lay back against the pillows with a feeling of miserable uncertainty. Would she ever see him again? She ought not to care. If he were through with her, it was only because she had refused him something more than he had a right to ask. She would be well rid of him. But logic had no power to relieve the pain that stabbed her.

She didn't want to be rid of him. The first chords of life's great symphony sounded in her heart. What was the use of denying that she loved him? She could keep it a secret from others. The last to learn of it would be Don himself. But in the cloister of her thoughts, deception was impossible. Indeed, she had no wish to deceive herself. The song of songs was intoxicatingly sweet. It bore her spirit off on the wings of morning.

LOVE'S GREATEST MISTAKE 21

Nor he with her! Some day he would marry an heiress in New York. She had lost him by her conduct at Troup's. She was glad of it!

While this sophistry was still crying down the small, anguished voice in Honey's heart, Jane awakened and sat up in bed.

"What time is it?" she asked, blinking; then glanced at the clock for her answer.

"When did *you* get home?" Honey said, jumping up and raising the shades. A flood of sunlight poured in.

"About five. Mr. Kendall took me to get something to eat—at Child's. I like him."

"I noticed you did. You took him away from me fast enough."

"Really? I didn't mean to. He just—stuck around. I don't think he's very happy."

"No?" Honey laughed. "He told me he wasn't. That's just his line, I guess. I'm surprised, *your* falling for him."

"Who says I've fallen for him? Don't be silly. I said I liked him. I do. He's gay and bright and—good looking. Of course, I love George, but for all I get out of life I might just as well be one of his washing-machines. He's happy as long as he has a 'nice little home,' as he calls it, to come back to. Men like George never think a woman might want a bit of romance occasionally."

Honey sat on the edge of the bed, staring out of the window. A row of althæa bushes screened it. George had planted them. "A nice little home." It was that—small, clean, bright—with a mortgage installment to be paid each month. George Sommers had worked hard for his home. He liked it—spent most of his Sundays fussing over it, painting, planting, putting up screens, awnings, getting rid of weeds.

But, like most men, he took his wife entirely for granted. To have put his arms around her, complimented her on her looks, kissed her, would have seemed to him silly. They had been married for five years. Life would go on just so, indefinitely. "A nice little home." Very remote from the hot breath of the jungle.

"Look at mother and father," Jane went on, interrupting Honey's thoughts. "Just automatons. Father works for the 'party,' and feels complimented when Pat Kennedy gives him a twenty-five-cent cigar. He isn't well—you know that. Been talking about a sea trip, a long rest, for twenty years; but he's never got it—never will. As for mother, she's just dried

LOVE'S GREATEST MISTAKE 23

up. All that life means to her is the hereafter.

"Don't talk to me about homes. If Don Kendall interests, amuses me, where's the harm in it? With you it's different. I kept him away from you on purpose. With your looks there's no reason why you shouldn't marry a rich husband. A woman with money never needs to be bored. But don't waste your time on Don Kendall. He isn't the marrying kind. Now, take that young Mr. Gibbs—"

"Oh, piffle!" Honey exclaimed, and, going into the bathroom, turned on the faucets. Jane was still talking, but the noise of the water drowned her words.

It was noon when the two girls finally breakfasted. There had been a telephone call for Jane, but she had answered in monosyllables, and had offered no explanation. When Honey rose to go, her sister made no attempt to detain her. She had housework to do, she said.

Just as Honey, after walking a block down Oak Avenue, was turning the corner of Maple, she saw Don Kendall's roadster flash by and presently stop in front of her sister's door. A twinge of jealousy went through her. So *that* had been the meaning of the telephone call. She could not know that Don had inquired first of all for her; had asked if she was in.

So Honey walked on, anger and a little bewilderment in her heart.

CHAPTER IV

It was a week after the Troup party when Honey, going into Harrison's drug store for an ice-cream soda, happened to meet her friend, Sally Terry.

The two girls had gone to school together, and later Sally's older sister, Mona, had achieved some notoriety by departing for New York in the company of a cloak-and-suit salesman she had "picked up" in the Penn House lobby. Now she was reported to be prospering famously as a model.

Sally, being a movie fan, suggested a picture. Once in their seats, she talked incessantly through a dull comedy while waiting for the feature to come on. Sally had a way of airing her views on life as she saw it through the medium of sex magazines, Sunday supplements, and motion pictures. Honey laughed at some of her views, but found most of them interesting. She asked the girl about Mona.

"I don't blame her a bit," Sally said, her

beady brown eyes narrowed rebelliously. "I'd like to get out of this one-horse town myself. Talk about virtue! It's the bunk. Who's wearing the pearls these days? Dutiful wives sitting home darning socks? Sweet girl graduates making fudge for Sunday-school picnics? Don't make me laugh.

"I tell you, Honey, it pays to advertise. Take Doris Doronda—there on the screen. Five years ago she was punching the cash register in a Chicago candy shop. Now she's worth millions. How do you suppose she did it? By saving up all the nice little pennies she had left over from her salary every Saturday night? Huh! They say her marble swimming-pool in Hollywood cost twenty thousand.

"If I could get away with anything like that, you wouldn't catch me worrying about being good.

" 'Being good'—do *you* know what it is? I don't. Mother thinks it's going to church. Wonder what she'd say if I told her one of the deacons at the Union Memorial tried to make a date with me last week? What do *you* think about this virtue thing?" She gave Honey a quick stare.

Honey's thoughts flew to Don Kendall.

"To me it's something like keeping your self-respect," she answered slowly.

"That's all the bunk, too," Sally sputtered. "I haven't heard of any of these dames we read about on the front page dying of remorse."

When Honey got home that afternoon she found Herbert Gibbs just driving up to the door. It was the first time she had seen him since the party. He had been in New York, he explained, and was on the point of returning there. Now that the new City Hall was well under way, the work of inspection could be carried on by one of his assistants.

Honey invited him into the dim little parlor filled with the odors of lamb stew. Gibbs, it seemed, had called to say good-by—to give Honey his address in case she should ever come to New York. He wanted to see more of her—would like to show her around.

"I've got a little apartment on Fifty-eighth Street," he told her; "but my real home is up in Connecticut, near Stamford. That's where mother and my two sisters live. I should like to have you meet them. The old place is charming. Beautiful trees and lawns—shrubbery. And some lovely old furniture my mother takes great pride in.

"My older sister, Josie, is a regular home body, like mother. 'Lovey,' the other one, is different. She'd like to go on the stage, I guess—do something. You'd like Lovey. Everybody does. Having my work, of course, I can sympathize with her. One reason I have to go back is, I'm submitting designs for a new church building in Washington. Working on the plans now. It's a competition. If I win it I'll be made for life."

"How exciting!" Honey said; but she was not really excited.

"I've read a lot about the supper clubs and cabarets in New York," she added. "And the places that keep open all night, though it's against the law. They must be wonderful."

Gibbs exhibited no enthusiasm.

"Sucker joints," he answered. "Filled with butter-and-egg men from out of town. Real New Yorkers never go to them, unless they happen to be showing some friend the sights. I could take you, of course, if you wanted to go."

He seemed a trifle disappointed, and Honey, who really liked him in a friendly sort of way, and who wanted to keep his friendship, gave him one of her most provocative smiles.

"We might try it just once," she said, "if I ever get to New York. And I'd love to meet your mother and sisters."

Under the warmth of her smile Gibbs instantly revived. It seemed to Honey that she really had made a deep impression on him. When he left, and they stood for a moment in the shadowy front hall, she pressed his hand and smiled at him again, whereupon Mr. Gibbs promptly kissed her. It was a clumsy kiss. She wiped it away when his back was turned. Don Kendall would have done better. But—there might be such a thing as knowing how to kiss too well.

CHAPTER V

As Honey set the table for supper, she tried to imagine herself married to Herbert Gibbs, as Jane had suggested. A nice little home in the suburbs—like Jane's perhaps, only larger—with Herbert coming home to plant rose bushes and ivy. Children—he had told her he loved children. His trips away. Waiting for him to return. Food. Sleep.

Was that life? Jane had said it wasn't. There might be something in Sally Terry's ideas, after all. To live perilously—dangerously!

She would not live cheaply, meanly, in a continual round of household drudgery. The price of that decision could be—whatever it was to be! Men were either cads, like Don, or narrow, self-centered dumb-bells, like Herbert Gibbs!

They either wanted to marry you, and make a servant or an article of furniture out of you; or else they wanted to have their selfish way about things and disappear. Women were honorable; men were dishonorable, selfish beasts.

If a woman loved a man, she wanted to make him happy; to see him get ahead in the world—amount to something in the estimation of other men. But men weren't like that. They were always thinking about themselves, their comforts, whatever fitted most smoothly into their schemes of life.

George ought to know that Jane was unhappy. Why didn't he do something about it? Were women the only ones with eyes that could see romance, glamour, gayety—and all the other really worth-while things of life?

The smell of the Irish stew suffocated her. The cheap window curtains hung in sleazy, unlovely folds. Many flies had crept through the worn-out screens.

Her father, under the influence of several drinks of bad gin, was holding forth on his usual topic—his need of a long rest, the general hopelessness of his dull existence.

Her mother's thin, bloodless lips, tightly compressed, seemed to say, "This world is a vale of sorrow; prepare for the life to come."

"Sam Dutcher was telling me today," her father was saying in his high-pitched, complaining voice, "that I don't look well. I ought to take a sea trip or something. Wish to God I could!"

The poor soul had needed that trip for twenty-five years, and had got no farther than Coney Island. Now the brave spirit of adventure in him had died down to a tiny flame. It flickered up momentarily when he saw pictures of far-away places, of rock-bound shores and blue lagoons; but it was a very faint flicker indeed, soon extinguished by the odors of Irish stew.

Mrs. McNeill called these spells "booze dreams," and told him he ought to think more about his future. As if he had any future other than to feed worms! His soul—and certainly he must once have had one—was petrified—dead. Somewhere within him a faint echo of life resounded; but it was only an echo—the hollow beat of a drum.

"That Mr. Gibbs seems a nice young man," Mrs. McNeill mumbled. She had glimpsed him through the front window. "He looks serious—not like most of the young fellows you meet nowadays, with their pockets full of gin. If he took a fancy to you, Honey, he might make you a good husband."

"I don't want a good husband," Honey said

spitefully. "Or any husband. I want to go to work."

"Work!" Her mother made the word seem almost immoral. "A woman's place is in the home. You should marry, Honey, and settle down, like Jane. She's happy with George. He's honest, reliable, hard working."

Honey thought of her sister's talk that morning after the party. Was the whole world mad? Her mother made no pretense to being happy. Nor did Jane. Was it not possible, in some way, to be free? Was one necessarily damned for not thinking forever of the conventions?

She spent the evening reading a magazine, wishing she were with Don Kendall.

He might be dangerous, but he was at least amusing. Merely to think of him thrilled her oddly. Of the men she knew, he alone suggested the cavalier. The others were all Puritans and shopkeepers in their hearts. They would grow to be big thread-and-button men; they would join chambers of commerce, and refer to the women who loved them as "the wife" or "the little woman."

Dan was a reprobate, perhaps. He might attempt to drag her in the dirt. (And she toyed with that idea a moment. It *would* be exciting!) But if he dragged her down he could also lift her up—which was more than anyone else could do!

She asked herself how much she would concede to him in some accidentally transcendent moment—if, for example, they were facing death together, or were cast away upon an island, beyond the possibility of rescue.

The extent to which her imagination carried her made her leap to her feet, turn aside from her mirror, and cast herself upon her bed. There her fingers knotted themselves into her pillow and her body shook in an inexplicable hysteria of rage and pain.

She hated him! He had no right to disrupt her life. He had gone back to New York—without even having telephoned her. Very well! She was glad of it! She hoped she would never see him again! There were other interesting men in the world. There must be. She'd find one, if she hunted to the end of the earth.

She found her magazine, flung herself into a chair, opened it, and stared at the type.

At last she gave up the pretense of reading and went back to her bed. But in the darkness the courage of her rebellion seemed to fade away. She felt alone—tragically alone—and with the sleep that crept over her came a strange dread, a sense that the rushing emotions of the last few days were wild currents in a stream of fate, which had snatched her up and were carrying her relentlessly toward a crisis she could not escape.

CHAPTER VI

Honey, reaching home after a stroll with Jane the following afternoon, found a house of dreadful turmoil. Her father had collapsed suddenly in his office an hour before—had been brought home dead. Life's problems, as far as he was concerned, were all solved—ended.

She sat in her room for many hours, weeping, wondering what the future held in store for them now. Their home, no doubt, would be broken up. There would be no money with which to run it now. She would have to go to work, of course, and that knowledge she welcomed.

But to find work—that was the problem; work that would mean even a bare living. She would doubtless be obliged to spend the years of her youth over a typewriter—unless she happened to marry some hard-working, honest man, as Jane had done.

A fortune teller had once predicted that she would marry millions. Honey did not know any millionaires—never expected to know any

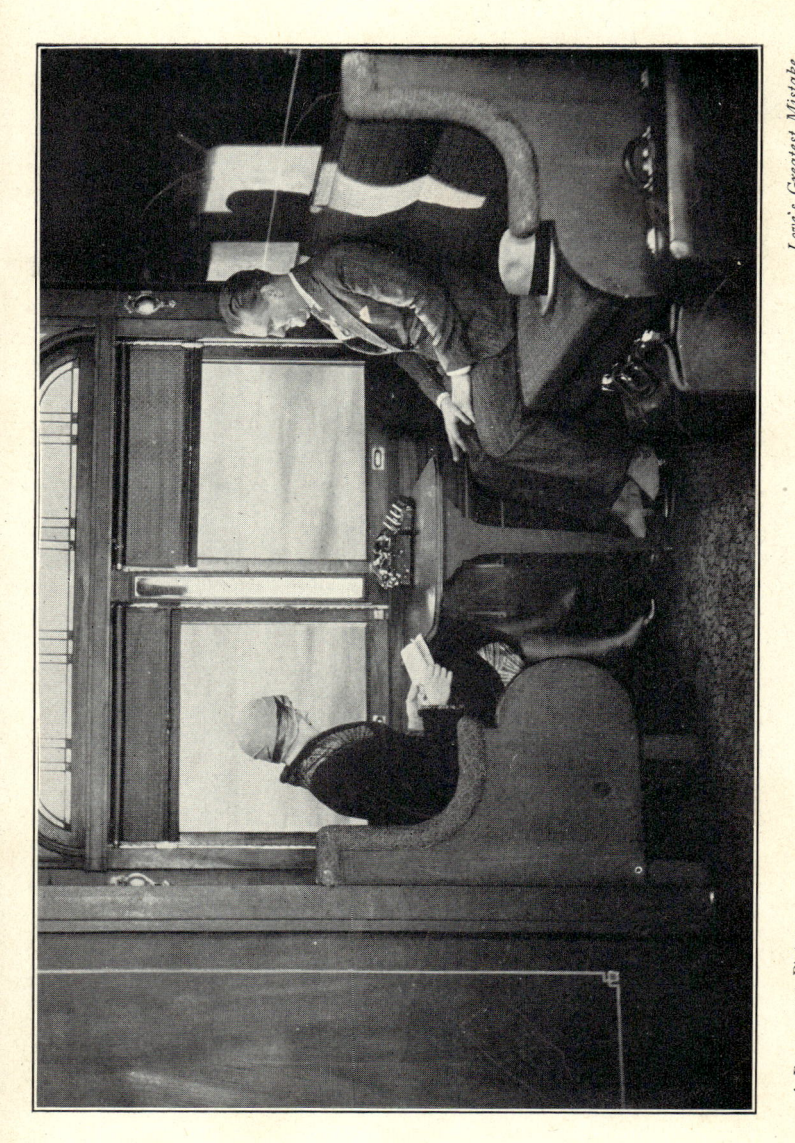

A Paramount Picture. *Love's Greatest Mistake.*
HONEY MEETS THE RICH WILLIAM OGDEN ON A PULLMAN TRAIN.

—except Don Kendall. He was one—or would be some day.

As if in response to her thoughts, she heard Jane calling softly to her, telling her she was wanted on the telephone.

She was amazed to hear Don's voice, warm, deep, sympathetic.

"I've just heard the terrible news, Honey," he said. "I want to let you know how shocked I am—how deeply I sympathize with you in your trouble. Is there anything I can do? If there is, just tell me, dear. Anything."

Honey thanked him through choking tears. There was a sincerity in his voice that seemed, in her grief, almost a caress. A big-brother caress, no doubt, but still very sweet. The mere fact that he had called at all was sweet. The thought of it was to cheer her through many bitter days.

At 5 o'clock on the day of Mr. McNeill's funeral, the McNeill family, including the in-laws, sat in ostentatiously solemn conclave around the dining-room table in the little house on Grove Street.

The funeral had taken place at 12 o'clock. Poor Mr. McNeill had made no vivid impression on the world during his lifetime, and his

38 LOVE'S GREATEST MISTAKE

departure was now forgotten in an argument over what to do with the $10,000 of life insurance left by the deceased.

Mrs. McNeill, rather dowdy in a hastily constructed black silk, wanted to use the money to buy the house on which they had been paying rent for twenty years, in order that she might go on living in what had become her home. She loved it as one loves a habit, which was natural enough.

Martin, her son, who lived in Philadelphia and operated a small milk route, objected violently.

"What would you live on?" he asked in a loud, unpleasant voice. "It's absurd."

"I thought I might take in boarders," the old lady quavered. "With Honey to help me—"

"No good. Put the money in my business. I need it, to expand. Grace and I"—he turned to his plump and brainless wife—"will take you to live with us—give you a nice home. That's what you ought to do."

"But—what about Honey?"

"Honey can go to work. Time she did, anyway."

"I think it would be much better," Jane

Sommers broke in, "for mother to invest the money in safe bonds. George says she can get six per cent—that's six hundred a year. Then she and Honey can come and live with us. Pay a small board, of course—enough to cover expenses. There's plenty of room."

Jane looked very smart in her mourning.

"Very nice for you and George," Martin sneered.

"No nicer than for you to use the money in your old business."

"I do think Honey should do something," Grace remarked in her vapid voice. "I did, until Martin married me. Do now, in fact—take care of my home. That's work enough for any woman, I can tell you."

"I don't approve of young girls going into business," Mrs. McNeill announced. "They never did in my time. Honey's place is with me—till she marries some hard-working young man and settles down in a nice little home."

Up to this point Honey herself had said nothing. She had, however, been doing a great deal of thinking.

"It seems to me," she remarked, "that you are all settling my affairs for me in a very high-handed way. Don't forget I'm free and white, and if I'm not twenty-one, still I'm of age and can do as I please."

"And what do you please?" Martin inquired sarcastically. He had never, at any time, been overfond of his younger sister.

"I haven't decided yet. I think I'll go to New York and look for a job."

"Doing what?" Again Martin sneered. "There's twenty thousand girls walking Broadway right now, looking for jobs. Maybe you figure you'll be a movie queen or something."

"Something, anyhow." Honey's face was pink with anger, now. "Something worth while. I'll never do that, sitting around this one-horse town. I won't help mother run a boarding-house—that's flat. If you ask me, I think Jane's suggestion is the best. Let mother put her money in bonds. Then she'll have it and maybe fifty dollars a month— enough to pay her board. If she divides her time between you two"—she included her brother and sister in a glance—"you'll each get some of her income, which I guess is what you want.

"But leave me out. I've been practicing on that old typewriter dad brought home from the office last summer, and I'm pretty good at it. You can scrap all you like over dad's life insurance—I don't want any of it."

Honey rose and flounced out of the room, which broke up the conference. The rent for the house, it happened, had been paid only two days before, which gave Mrs. McNeill her home for another month at least. In the interim, it was agreed that the life-insurance money was to be placed in the bank, along with some other small savings Mrs. McNeill had made "to be buried with."

Honey went out to the front porch and stood there, breathing in the clear air. The atmosphere of the house had almost suffocated her.

Then the lights of a car flashed into the gloomy little street—Don Kendall's car, as she realized to her amazement when she saw him advancing rapidly up the brick-paved front walk.

"Hello, Honey child," he said in his low, deep voice. "I hope I'm not intruding at a time like this, but I thought maybe, for an hour, you might like to—to get some air." He waved toward the parked roadster.

Honey touched his hand with her small, cold fingers, went swiftly down the path with him.

She did not even think about stopping to get her hat. Don held open the door of the car with the grace of a courtier. How different he seemed from the primitive, passionate creature of a few nights before! Now he was a dear, understanding friend. Silent, cool, stern almost, he drove the car along deserted roads at tremendous speed, so that Honey had the sensation of being in an airplane, flying.

"I thought you had gone back to New York," she ventured.

"Going tomorrow," he told her, without explanation or comment. Then silence.

A strange ride, Honey thought. But in a way she understood it. Don was apologizing for what had happened at Mr. Troup's party by treating her as a friend—a little girl friend in trouble. Before, he had treated her as a woman—almost as his woman.

When, an hour later, he waved her a courteous good night, she went into the house curiously sad.

CHAPTER VII

ONE morning some two weeks later Jane arrived at the house in a state of great excitement. Assisted by Honey, Mrs. McNeill was washing the breakfast dishes, indulging meanwhile in a running monologue on the virtues of her late husband, telling Honey for the hundredth time how sorry she was that "Pop" had never taken his long-dreamed-of trip.

Jane burst in, waving a letter.

"I've just heard from George!" she cried. "He's in New York. They sent for him—from the home office. He's going to get a big raise. And new territory: Connecticut—Rhode Island —northern New York. They want him to travel from there. We'll have to sell the bungalow and move. Isn't that simply wonderful?"

"Give up your home?" Mrs. McNeill asked. "Why, George could be here, just the same, when he's off the road. I think it's foolish."

Honey wondered a little at her sister's excitement. Since the morning after the party at Ben Troup's, when she had seen Don Kendall drive up in his car to Jane's door, Honey had never asked any questions concerning that young man, and her sister had offered no confidences. Nevertheless, Honey had often wondered whether Mr. Kendall had continued his visits to the bungalow on Oak Avenue. A childish jealousy on her part, perhaps, yet it persisted.

Whenever she had seen Jane lately, Honey noticed that her sister spoke of a desire to "run up to New York for a few days," ostensibly to "do a little shopping." But the money required for even a short stay in the metropolis was beyond George Sommers' means; so Jane had taken out her trip in talking. Now came the prospect of actually moving to New York.

"Won't it be wonderful, Honey?" Jane chattered on. "You say you want to get a job. New York's the place to find one. George and I will probably take a cunning little apartment, and you can come and visit us. No trouble to sell the bungalow. Pierce and Stratton, the real-estate people, had an offer for it only last month. We'd take our furniture, of course. And mother could go to Philadelphia and stay with Martin and his wife. They'd be tickled

LOVE'S GREATEST MISTAKE 45

to death to have her, on account of the board. I'm so excited I can hardly talk."

"Have you heard from Don Kendall lately?" Honey asked, when Mrs. McNeill had retired to her armchair on the back porch.

Jane gave her sister a cool stare.

"Why do you ask me that?" she replied.

"Why not?" Honey countered. "You were tremendously interested in him, weren't you?"

"Mr. Kendall and I are very good friends. I like him very much. And I have had a couple of letters from him, since you ask me. What of it?"

"Nothing. I just wondered. I had a note from Mr. Gibbs—you remember him, don't you?—asking me, in case I came up to town, to let him know."

"Gibbs? Oh—that tall, serious, near-sighted young man with the glasses. I thought him very nice, myself. When you come to visit me, you can look him up."

"Is it all settled, then? You're really going?"

"Certainly. George doesn't know it yet, but he will when he gets back Saturday night. I've already spoken to the real-estate people about the house. Why on earth should I waste my

46 LOVE'S GREATEST MISTAKE

life here in this miserable little place when I can step out in a real city? Nice little homes may be all very well, but what do they get you? What did living here ever get mother? Or father?"

When Jane had gone, Honey went to her room, lifted the cover from the battered machine, and wrote:

DEAR DON:

I cannot tell you how much I appreciated your call before you went back to New York. I may be coming up to town myself very soon, and it would be nice to see you. I'll be staying with my sister, who is planning to take an apartment there. If I do come, I'll let you know the address. Good-by, and I do hope you haven't forgotten all about me.
HONEY.

Jane Sommers, now that opportunity presented itself, acted with characteristic energy. A For Sale sign bloomed against the front of the bungalow overnight—along with the althæas. An early-morning train took her to New York for a conference with George. The latter, overpowered by his sudden good fortune, did no conferring. He merely listened while Jane told him what they were going to do.

LOVE'S GREATEST MISTAKE 47

The very next day, after hours spent in a taxicab with a real-estate agent, going the rounds of available apartments, she found what she wanted—a four-room, kitchenette, and bath flat, two flights up, without an elevator, on Eighty-second Street, at a monthly rental that made her open her eyes very wide indeed, but that was still within the prescribed one-third of George's new income. Two weeks later she was settled in it.

Meanwhile Honey, helping her mother in the daily and dull routine of running the house, was tremendously happy. They lived in an atmosphere of gloom. Now that Mr. McNeill's pay check had been cut off along with Mr. McNeill himself, they were living on principal—nibbling the edges, as it were, of the $10,000 of life insurance that her father had left. There had been other nibbles to settle Mr. McNeill's unpaid bills—not large, but still cruelly visible on the bank statements.

About the middle of the second month following Jane's departure, Honey received a letter from her brother Martin.

I am surprised [he wrote] that you are willing to go on living on your widowed mother. Before long her little bit of money will be used up. In my business I could have doubled it. Now that Jane and George have gone to New York, mother's place is here with me. As her son, I am the head of the family. Why don't you go out and find something to do? You ought to be ashamed of yourself.

Honey finished reading the letter, crimson with indignation. She had told her mother a hundred times in the past few weeks that she wanted to go to work, and each time the old lady had begun to weep that it was selfish and inhuman on Honey's part even to suggest abandoning her mother, now that she was left alone in the world with no one to look after her. All of which was highly illogical, but had a definite reason behind it. Mrs. McNeill loved her home. It was like an old shoe. The mere thought of being deprived of it terrified her.

She was sitting in her favorite rush-bottomed chair, gazing out at the flaming hollyhocks and dreaming, no doubt, of a cherished past, when Honey, her cheeks flushed, her eyes blazing with determination, swept into the room.

"Why, dear child!" exclaimed her mother.

"What's wrong? What's the matter? You look so—so excited. So lovely."

Honey did not notice the unaccustomed compliment. With a fine gesture she tossed the letter from her brother into Mrs. McNeill's lap.

"Read that!" she exclaimed.

Mrs. McNeill fumbled with her spectacles, but Honey continued:

"Martin says I ought to be ashamed of myself, sponging on you this way. He says we are using up your little bit of principal, and that I ought to go to work. I think he's right. I'm leaving for New York tomorrow. I'll stay with Jane until I get something to do. She told me I could. Martin says Grace will come over from Philadelphia and help you straighten things out—get rid of the house. You're going to live with them, in Philadelphia. We certainly can't drift on this way. I've known that all along."

"But, child," Mrs. McNeill began, her voice thick with tears, "I can't let a young girl like you go to that wicked city—"

"Oh, piffle!" Honey sat on the edge of the kitchen table, waving her charming legs. "New York isn't a bit more wicked than any other place. I'm sick of all this nonsense. I'm going out right now and send a wire to Martin to have Grace here tomorrow. And as soon as she gets here I leave.''

She dashed out of the room, leaving poor Mrs. McNeill gazing helplessly into space and gasping.

Honey, in an interval of packing, gazed around her roomy old bedroom. The pink-and-cream-striped wall paper was old and spotted, but she had been familiar with it since childhood. Two windows faced the side yard, with its row of lilac bushes. Two more overlooked the roof of the front porch facing Grove Street. Rusty green shades cut off the view in both directions. They were drawn, because it was night.

She had just finished reading an article in a magazine that Sally Terry had left her, entitled, How to Get On in the World. A girl, the article said, is not only justified but required to make use of her sex appeal in order to get along—to succeed—in the workaday world.

Why was it not as reasonable, the writer of the article argued, for a woman to use her charm to secure a business engagement as it was to secure a husband? It was to the woman

LOVE'S GREATEST MISTAKE

It amazed her to find herself thinking so much about Don. Certainly he was not thinking about her. She pictured him in New York, making his gay round of the theaters and the cabarets, amusing himself nightly with a different woman. She hated him—she loved him. She never wanted to see him again—she wished for him from minute to minute, childishly, innocently, yet with a very real longing. In the end she turned off the lights and, throwing herself on the bed, buried her face in the pillows.

CHAPTER VIII

WHEN Honey settled into her seat in the Pullman car, she saw that the chair next to hers had been turned to face her, but it was unoccupied. She had decided against the day coach because it seemed worth the small extra fare to make her journey to New York a triumphal shaking of the dust of her home town from her feet.

She gazed at the chair opposite her, wondering who would come to occupy it. A cane and a light overcoat in the rack above, a costly English kit bag on the floor, gave evidence that the seat was taken. Her neighbor no doubt was enjoying a cigar in the smoking compartment.

Honey was thinking idly of these not very important matters when a man came along the aisle behind her and sank into the seat.

The impression she received was instantly one of wealth—wealth and breeding. They seemed to radiate from him.

Honey could not decide whether he was in

LOVE'S GREATEST MISTAKE 55

his late forties or his early fifties. She examined him critically without appearing to do so, then began to glance through a magazine. Whereupon her vis-à-vis undertook an equally critical examination of herself.

Then he spoke, just as Honey had felt sure he would—in a cool, pleasant, rather deep voice.

"On your way to New York?" he asked.

"Why—yes," Honey stammered. "And for the first time, too. I'm terribly excited."

"I suppose so. Naturally. Well, you have many interesting experiences ahead of you. Visiting friends, I suppose?"

There was a very friendly quality in his smile.

"Yes. In a way. I'm going to stay with my married sister for a while, until I find something to do—work, you know. She has an apartment on Eighty-second Street."

"So you are looking for work, are you? Well, it's quite the thing for women to do nowadays. If I am not too curious, what sort of work have you in mind?"

"Oh—anything to make a living. I'm a fairly good typist, but that's all."

"Not quite all—not by any means."

56 LOVE'S GREATEST MISTAKE

The man's eyes were dancing with humor as they swept from Honey's lovely face to the alluring curves of her legs. She was glad, now, that she had worn her new gray chiffon stockings.

"You mean—things that would help me in making a living?" Honey asked, remembering the article she had read the night before, in which women were told to use their good looks to achieve success in the world.

"Why not?" he laughed. "I have always maintained that charm in a woman is an asset in business. I have quite a number of employees around me, and I find that a well groomed, attractive office force is pleasanter to work with—to have about. Beauty in our daily life is an asset. We do not have enough of it."

Honey gave her companion a sudden brilliant smile, her long lashes fluttering.

"It's nice of you to think me good-looking," she whispered, so that the severe-looking dowager across the aisle could not hear. "You must have seen so many women—"

"Not many," her companion answered, leaning forward in his chair, "so good-looking as you."

"Really?" Honey murmured, coloring a

LOVE'S GREATEST MISTAKE 57

little under his direct gaze. "That's one of the very nicest things I ever heard. Especially coming from you."

"Why from me especially?"

"Because I can see—I can tell at once—that—that you are a man who has seen everything. The kind of a man who knows women. A man of the world."

With Honey this was not flattery. She felt it—meant it.

Her companion drew out a wafer-thin watch.

"Don't you think it would be nice, Miss—"

"McNeill," Honey supplied. "Margaret McNeill. But everybody calls me Honey."

"Really! Delightful. Most appropriate, too, I must say. 'Honey?' Well, since you say everyone calls you that, I hope you won't mind if I do so, too. What I was about to suggest, Honey,"—he spoke the name in a way that made it seem almost a caress—"was that it is time for lunch, and, as I particularly dislike to eat alone, it would give me a great deal of pleasure to have you join me."

Honey glanced down at her satchel, in which lay the sandwiches her mother had prepared for her. She knew, without looking, that the

58 LOVE'S GREATEST MISTAKE

prim lady across the aisle was regarding her with a contemptuous frown.

"Why—I—really, Mr.—" she stammered.

"My name is Ogden—William Ogden." He took out a small gold case and presented Honey with a card. "It really would be a favor on your part to have luncheon with me. Won't you?"

His voice, his manner, held a certain sincerity, a frankness, that impressed Honey deeply. There was no doubt about it, Mr. Ogden was a very charming man—in spite of his age; perhaps even because of it. He did not lose by it, certainly—in a way, it made him more attractive. Honey could not help feeling that anything he did would be suavely, perfectly done. There seemed no good reason for refusing his luncheon invitation.

"Why, Mr. Ogden, I'd love it," she said, rising from her seat.

Over the little swaying table they became more intimate. Mr. Ogden questioned her, in a pleasantly interested way, about her home, her parents, her future plans, and suggested that if Honey would look him up at his office he might be able to do something for her. He also mentioned the fact that he lived on East

LOVE'S GREATEST MISTAKE 59

Sixty-eighth Street, but that his wife, who was something of an invalid, spent a great deal of time at their country place in Southampton.

Mr. Ogden explained all this in a light and almost casual way that put Honey quite at her ease. With equal casualness he mentioned that during the summer his town house was closed, and that he lived at his club, running down to Southampton for the week-ends. This, he explained, made his existence rather a monotonous one.

"You can't imagine," he said, "how dull the evenings are, at times, for an old fellow like myself." He said this in a way that showed he did not consider himself old at all. "Nowhere to go—nothing to do—no one to play around with—"

"You don't seem old to me, at all," Honey told him.

"Well, nowadays, when a man gets to be around fifty, the rising generation considers him antiquated," he laughed. "Although I think I could outstep a great many of these youngsters at that. But my evenings are dull. Take tonight, for example. We get in around five. I go to my club, dress for dinner, have a cocktail. Then what? A stupid meal some-

60 LOVE'S GREATEST MISTAKE

where—alone. The theater—also alone, or with some fellow from the club. I hate it.

"Look here, Honey, why not take pity on me, cheer me up for the evening? I'll bet you haven't a thing to do. And I'll guarantee to deliver you at your sister's apartment, safe and sound, right after the theater. Unless you might want to have a bit of dinner first. No reason why she should mind, is there?"

Honey shook her head. This was going much too fast.

"My sister is to meet me at the train," she said. "She's expecting me. And if I appeared with you she might want to know—"

"Of course," Mr. Ogden interrupted, still with his pleasantly humorous smile. "I'm disappointed, of course. We'll do it some other time. Promise me that, won't you?"

"Certainly," Honey said. "I'd love it."

When she left him at the foot of the iron stairway in the Pennsylvania Station, it was with a promise to see him again—to call him up.

In the pocket of her coat she felt the card he had given her. She took it out for a moment, glanced at it. Being a personal card, it carried no address, but Honey knew she

LOVE'S GREATEST MISTAKE 61

could readily find his number in the telephone directory. Was it worth while? Had not the man merely tried to "pick her up"?

She was about to tear the card in two, throw it away, dismiss the whole matter from her mind, when she remembered the purpose of her visit to New York—to obtain work at any cost, and soon.

Honey stood undecided at the foot of the stairway, the card in her hand, her satchel on the floor beside her. Then she turned the bit of pasteboard over. On its reverse side Mr. Ogden had written, in pencil, the words:

Admit Miss McNeill at any time. W. O.

Was not this her golden opportunity—her chance to win success? With a lift of her chin, she thrust the card into her pocket and, taking up her satchel, began to mount the stairs.

CHAPTER IX

WHEN Honey caught sight of Jane standing at the head of the stairway in the Pennsylvania Station, she was amazed at the change that a few weeks in New York had made in her sister.

Jane had always dressed well—as well as her limited purse would allow—but now there was a new and noticeable smartness about her —the smartness of Fifth Avenue, of Broadway. Honey had not failed to observe this in the clothes of her chance acquaintance of the train, Mr. William Ogden, whose card now lay in her pocket.

"Why—hello, sis!" she exclaimed. "You're positively stunning. I love your coat. Oh— where *did* you get that dream of a wrist watch? George must certainly be making lots of money these days."

"George is doing very well," Jane replied, a faint frown around her cool gray-blue eyes. "He earns a good deal on commissions. But

LOVE'S GREATEST MISTAKE 63

these things aren't as expensive as they look. Just—smart; in good taste. All a woman needs in New York, to look well nowadays, is good taste. The shops are wonderful—full of all sorts of bargains, if you take the trouble to hunt for them."

"That wrist watch doesn't look like a bargain," Honey laughed. "Platinum, isn't it? Or white gold? Set with diamonds, too!"

"They aren't diamonds; they're rhinestones. And it isn't platinum. Just a plated affair I picked up at a sale the other day." She drew the sleeve of her coat down over her wrist. "For heaven's sake, Honey, don't get so excited over a few bits of finery. New York women all try to look as well as they can. It's part of the game. Where's your trunk check? We'd better attend to that right away. Then we'll get a cab." She signaled a porter to take charge of Honey's satchel. "Have a pleasant trip?"

Honey nodded without mentioning her meeting with Mr. Ogden. She meant to speak of that later. At the moment she was regarding with astonished eyes the immense waiting-room, the hurrying crowds, as she followed Jane and the porter to the cab stand. A few

64 LOVE'S GREATEST MISTAKE

minutes later they were on their way uptown.

Jane's apartment was a modest one, and to Honey, accustomed as she was to the spaciousness of the old-fashioned house back home, the rooms seemed particularly tiny. The bungalow furniture, however, had fitted in well, and with some new rugs and curtains Jane had managed to make the place very attractive. Honey was charmed with the little extra bedroom which was to be hers during her stay.

By the time she had unpacked her satchel Jane came to the door to tell her that dinner was ready.

"I guess we won't be going out tonight," she announced, when they had finished their meal and straightened up the kitchenette. "It's raining. And no doubt you're tired. I know I am. Didn't get to bed until after three."

She threw herself listlessly on the living-room couch and lighted a cigarette. It seemed to Honey that there were new and rather sad lines around her eyes.

"I suppose George is away," Honey said, perching herself in an easy chair, her legs dangling over its arm.

"Yes. This new territory they've given him

is larger and he has to make longer trips. I was out with—friends."

"I guess you've met a lot of people since you moved to New York."

"No, not many. Hardly any, in fact. You don't meet people in New York the way you do in smaller places. They all have their own friends and don't give a hang about strangers. If it hadn't been for Don Kendall—"

"Oh—you've seen him, then?" Honey's eyes grew wide.

"Of course I have. He's been very nice to me in lots of ways. If it hadn't been for him I'd have had a mighty dull time."

"I see." Honey felt a sudden pang of jealousy, and her eyes sought Jane's diamond-studded wrist watch, quite without reason.

"What are your plans about finding work?" Jane asked suddenly, as if she wished to change the subject. "Or have you any?"

"Well," Honey said, "there's George's company, of course. They might do something for me. I wrote you, you know, to have him speak to them."

"He did—the last time he was in town. The office manager said they had been laying off part of their force because some efficiency

66 LOVE'S GREATEST MISTAKE

expert was showing them how to save enough money to pay him his fee. Not much chance there, I'm afraid; although you might try."

Honey indulged in a rueful grin.

"So that's that. Well, there's Herbert Gibbs—the architect, you know. And Mona Terry."

"I don't think Mona is likely to be of any use to you. Not any good use, at least. She's —crooked."

"Well—a lot of people do things they shouldn't, I suppose," Honey said steadily, "but it's their business, not mine. If Mona Terry can help me find something to do, I'm not going to use a microscope on her morals. I don't have to be like her, do I?—unless I want to be."

"All right. Have it your own way. After all, you're in New York now, and must live your life to suit yourself. Nobody else can live it for you. I think it would be a mighty good idea to call up that Gibbs man in the morning. He's only a struggling young architect, but a girl can't have too many friends, if she wants to get anywhere in New York."

"Where's the telephone?" Honey asked suddenly.

LOVE'S GREATEST MISTAKE 67

"Over there." Jane waved her cigarette toward a small stand in the corner. "But you'd never be able to reach Mr. Gibbs now. It's half-past eight, and nobody in New York is ever in at such an hour, unless—"

"I wasn't going to call Mr. Gibbs," Honey interrupted. "I just wanted to look at the telephone book."

She came back to her chair with the heavy volume and began a careful search through the O's. Presently she found what she wanted. "William Ogden," she read, "Union Trust Building."

Jane was grinding the butt of her cigarette against an ash tray.

"Who's William Ogden?"

"A man I met on the train."

"Really! Somebody you picked up? I didn't suppose you went in for that sort of thing."

"Don't be silly, sis. Our seats were together and we just naturally talked. He's a rich man —and a very handsome and fascinating one— much older than I am—close to fifty, I should say."

"The worst kind."

"Maybe so. But, just the same, he has a

68 LOVE'S GREATEST MISTAKE

lot of people working for him, and said if I'd come to his office he'd see what he could do."

"Of course, he'll see what he can do. Better stay away."

"Then how am I ever going to get a position?"

"By going to office managers, people whose business it is to hire clerks—typists. Capitalists don't bother with such details, unless they have a reason. Take my advice and let Mr. Ogden alone. You won't get anywhere through him—not anywhere you want to get."

She spoke almost fiercely, as if Honey's morals, her virtue, must be protected at any cost.

"I appreciate the way you feel about me, Jane," Honey said gravely. "And I intend to take care of myself—don't worry about that. But, after all, while you're warning me against Mona Terry and Mr. Ogden, what about you and Don Kendall—"

"Don's just a friend," Jane interrupted sharply. "He amuses me. And I suppose I amuse him. Don't forget I'm a married woman, with a certain amount of freedom. You're not. And you never will be if you don't take care of your reputation. Once you've got a husband, it's different. And understand me: if I take dinner, go to a show, with another man once in a while—with Don, let us say— it doesn't mean that there's anything wrong about it, or that I love George any the less. But I'm human. I've got to have *somebody* to talk to now and then. If I didn't I'd go crazy."

"Does George know?" Honey asked.

"What? About Don?"

"Yes."

"No. Why should I tell him? It would only make him unhappy, and do nobody any good."

She spoke quickly, almost angrily, pacing up and down the little room—spoke as one on the defensive.

"My God, Honey, it was bad enough at home! Although I could run in and see you and mother—other friends—if I felt like it. But here—" She flung out her hands in a gesture of helplessness. "You'll find out too, before long, although you'll have work to occupy your mind during the day. I haven't—except to dust this little place every morning and fix myself something to eat. Ugh!" She shuddered. "Don't mind my ravings, child. I'm all shot to pieces tonight, as I told you, and I'm going to take a drink."

70 LOVE'S GREATEST MISTAKE

Jane took a bottle from one of the bookcase shelves, tilted it against the light.

"What's the idea?" Honey asked.

Jane found a glass and emptied the contents of the bottle into it.

"Well, I need it after dancing most of the night. You've got to take *something,* I suppose, here in New York, if you want to keep up the pace." She emptied the glass with a little shudder. "There; that will pull my nerves together—make me sleep. Shall we turn in?"

"I'm ready," Honey said. "I want to be full of pep tomorrow, when I start on the trail of that job. Good night."

She went to her room and undressed, but found, rather to her surprise, that she was not at all sleepy.

The window of her room faced the south, overlooking a sea of lights. Honey sat watching them, marveling at the glow that rose like a great white plume against the sky. The perpetual roar of the city seemed to stimulate her, to affect her nerves with a tingling sensation almost electrical.

Somewhere in all that maze of lights Don Kendall was no doubt pursuing his fascinating way. And Mr. Ogden. What had the latter decided to do, after her refusal to spend the evening with him?

She pictured him dining, going to the theater perhaps, with some charming woman. He knew plenty, of course, in spite of his talk about being lonely. This atmosphere of New York was *his* atmosphere.

Would she thrive in it, or would it suffocate her, as it seemed to be suffocating Jane? Honey began to perceive that she and Jane and Don and Mr. Ogden, and all the rest, were just queer little figures, puppets, dancing vainly through endless days and nights while Fate pulled the strings.

The thought did not please her. There must be some real purpose in the game of life. With a feeling of determination to find it, she took one last look at the roaring, many-lighted city, and, drawing down the window shade, went to bed.

CHAPTER X

When Honey telephoned Herbert Gibbs at his office the next morning, she knew from the sound of his voice that her call was a welcome one.

"Why, hello! This is great, your being in town," he said. "When did you get here? And how long are you going to stay?" Without waiting for an answer he went on: "What about taking dinner with me tonight—going to a show later? I've been working every evening his week so far, and I need a holiday."

"I think it would be wonderful," Honey said, and gave him Jane's address. "What time shall I expect you?"

"Oh—about half-past six. I'll try to get some seats for The Verdict. Great show. I've been wanting to see it for some time. You'll like it."

"I'm sure I will. And it's mighty sweet of you—"

"Not at all. Pleasure's mine. See you about six-thirty. 'By."

Jane, who had been listening to the conversation, was immediately full of plans for the evening. Did Honey have a suitable dress? She would furnish her with a latchkey, since she might be late getting home. Mr. Gibbs would, of course, want to have supper and dance after the theater. Everybody did.

Honey sat staring out of the window while her sister rattled on. She was thinking of Herbert Gibbs—wondering why, on the occasion of their earlier meetings, she had not particularly liked him—at least, had not been enthusiastic about him.

Jane was putting on her hat.

"Come along, sis," she said. "Let's take a run downtown. I've got some things to buy, and it will give you a chance to look about a little."

Not until Honey had gasped her way breathless through a two-hour experience in New York's retail shopping district did she remember that Mona Terry, her former schoolmate, worked in an exclusive little specialty shop just off Fifth Avenue. Sally, Mona's sister, had given her the address.

"Do you mind, Jane," she asked, "stopping in for a moment to see Mona Terry? She

74 LOVE'S GREATEST MISTAKE

works at Madame Valentine's. I know you don't approve of her, but she might help me to find something in the way of a position, just the same."

"All right." Jane glanced up at the street number. "It's five blocks up. Fortieth Street. Come along."

The very French young man who greeted them at Madame Valentine's lost interest when he discovered that they were not customers, but had come to see Miss Terry, one of the models.

"Since Mees Mona ees not engage, she will be permit to see you in ze dressing-room," he announced.

But a door that stood ajar at the rear of the shop was thrust open, and a mop of red hair appeared, above a piquant, defiant face and a gorgeous dressing-gown.

"Why—hello, Jane! Hello, Honey!" Miss Terry cried. "Sally wrote me you were coming. Step into my parlor, won't you?"

She pushed the door wide.

"Say, François"—she flashed a look at the young man—"forget the high-hat stuff when my friends call on me—see? 'Mees Mona will be permit' nothing! Anyway, it's my lunch

LOVE'S GREATEST MISTAKE 75

hour, isn't it? Go over in the corner and study your French dictionary."

Jane and Honey followed her into the small dressing-room.

"We can only stay a moment," Jane announced. She had never liked Mona and did not hesitate to show it.

"I stopped in to get your home address," said Honey. "Thought I might come and call on you some evening. Have a talk about the old town and all."

"Fine. I've got a dump on Madison near Thirty-sixth. Here." She took a card, scribbled the telephone number and the address. "Call me up any evening around six. Or drop in for a cocktail. How's the old burg getting along, anyway?"

"You haven't been back, have you?" Honey remarked.

"Not yet. But I'm going, some day. And when I do it'll be in a Rolls-Royce, you can gamble on that. They all said I'd go to the devil, didn't they? Well, I'll show them that if I do it won't be in a jitney. By-by. Look me up sometime, Honey."

She ushered them out, ignoring Jane completely.

"A bad egg," the latter snapped, when they were once more on the sidewalk.

"I think I'll go to see her, just the same," Honey said.

"Suit yourself. I wouldn't. It's getting late, and I'm hungry." Jane glanced at her wrist watch.

Honey was still wondering about that watch. Certainly the stones in it did not *look* like rhinestones.

The dining-room of the big hotel was bright and fairly well filled with guests, but somehow Honey did not find it gay. The sweep of tables, the excellent music, the subdued chatter, left her with a feeling of disappointment.

She had imagined a cozy, low-lit corner, a place designed for intimate confidences, for flirtation, even for love-making. How could two persons be intimate over a table in a dining-room as large as a convention hall?

Herbert apologized for not having arranged an intimate tête-à-tête; he had, he explained, been tremendously busy. The hotel, a new one on Park Avenue, was dignified, conservative— the sort of place to which a man could bring a "nice" girl. Honey reflected upon a certain sedate, old-fashioned quality in Herbert Gibbs,

LOVE'S GREATEST MISTAKE 77

while he carefully studied the menu. An earnest young man—there was no doubt of that; but did he ever "break loose"? As Don Kendall might break loose, for instance?

He had come for her in a cab, and talked to Jane for a few minutes in the living-room while Honey put the finishing touches to her toilette. When she appeared, wearing a gown of white chiffon over satin, which Jane had taken from her newly stocked wardrobe, Mr. Gibbs gave evidence, in a typically masculine way, that he considered her a dream of beauty.

They did not talk a great deal in the cab. At least, not after Honey had announced her purpose in coming to New York. Mr. Gibbs sat in silence for some time. The idea seemed to displease him.

"Awful pity," he said at length, "for a girl like you to have her youthful bloom rubbed off by contact with the business world. When a woman works, especially in the—er—less well paid capacities, she becomes—hard. Simply can't help it. She must, to hold her own. You are so sweet, so lovely, so—may I say?—innocent. It seems a shame."

Honey, eager for life and its keen contacts, shivered. Was the man going to treat her like a stained-glass angel? During dinner he talked at length of his work.

"There's a competition on," he explained to Honey, "for a new church—a sort of cathedral—in Washington. A ten-million-dollar job. I'm working on plans for it—nights, Sundays. Have been, for months. If I should be lucky enough to win it I'd be made for life. Famous all over the country. Wonderful, wouldn't it be? I've got so I think about the thing all the time—in my sleep, almost."

He drew a pencil from his pocket and sketched a Gothic window on the back of the menu.

Honey yawned. He had told her of this before. It was fine, of course, but—she wanted something else. Life. Passionate, throbbing life. To have dined in some gay place where one danced between courses. The sort of place to which Don Kendall would have taken her.

Well, there still remained the theater, with a possible supper afterward. One always danced at the supper places. Don had told her that. He had described the life of the night clubs in vivid detail.

"I couldn't get seats for The Verdict," Herbert explained, as he added up the dinner check.

LOVE'S GREATEST MISTAKE 79

"Eight weeks in advance. And nobody with any sense will pay the prices asked by the speculators—except visiting cloak-and-suit salesmen. So I thought you might like to see a movie. There's a new picture on at the Metropolitan. Jack Arlesworth in The Buccaneer. All the papers gave it splendid notices. We could get seats, I think, if we hurry." He tipped the waiter, glanced at his watch. "What do you say?"

What *could* she say, Honey thought, feeling rather limp. Eager for adventure, she felt like a runaway gypsy being taken on a Cook's tour. Everything seemed dull, flat, lacking in spice and savor. She followed Gibbs out of the restaurant in silence, got into the cab as if she were going to a funeral. Her companion, busy with his own thoughts, was unaware of her depression.

"I want you to meet my mother and sisters soon," he said. "I know you'll like them. We'll drive up some Sunday. The place is right near the water. You swim, don't you?"

"Yes," Honey said dully. She wondered what her companion really thought of her.

Herbert Gibbs, tremendously old-fashioned and serious, was at the moment revolving in his mind the idea that, as a hard-working young architect on a salary, he could not afford to marry; but that as the winner of a nation-wide competition, with large fees coming in as the work of construction progressed, matters would be entirely different.

"I'll have to take you home after the picture," he announced, "because the firm wants me to run up to New Haven tomorrow and I've got to make an early train. You won't mind, I hope. Next time we'll see a real show, and have supper afterward, and dance."

Honey's mind was far off—her feet beating to the throb of jungle music. "Next time?" She did not think there would be any "next time" for Mr. Gibbs and her. He was impossible, she decided; simply impossible.

She sat through the picture in silence, hating it. Hating him as well, which was quite unreasonable. Herbert Gibbs was not the first man to treat a woman as a saint and be thought a fool for his pains.

Yet Honey had no wish to be particularly unsaintlike. She was merely thinking what a different sort of evening she would have had with someone like—well, Mr. Ogden. Or Don Kendall. An evening of laughter—care-free, gay.

LOVE'S GREATEST MISTAKE 81

"I'm rather tired myself," she said truthfully. "And I couldn't think of keeping you up."

The sarcasm in her voice reached him.

"It's been a terribly dull evening for you, I know," he apologized, "but I'm not feeling well tonight. Been working too hard, I guess. Eight hours a day at the office—three or four every night at home—rather takes it out of you."

He gave her a tired smile, and Honey, glancing at his face, saw that it was pale and lined. A sudden wave of understanding came over her. Here was a man who was really trying to accomplish something big—something worth while. Perhaps the jazz-trotting youths of the cabarets might yet be working for him—asking him for jobs. She put out her hand, rested it softly for a moment on his.

A quick glow came into Herbert Gibbs' eyes as he felt the warm touch of her. The tension that gripped him relaxed.

"Honey," he said eagerly, "I can't begin to tell you how much I—like you. And I believe you *do* understand. I know the things you'd probably have enjoyed tonight. I've done them over and over. But somehow I can't exactly

82 LOVE'S GREATEST MISTAKE

picture you in the fast atmosphere of the night clubs, sitting alongside of bootleggers, gold-diggers, crooks. You seem so different—so—"

"Oh, Lord!" Honey thought. "Does he think I'm about to grow wings?" What she said was, "Suppose we go."

It was not yet eleven. A taxi whirled them to Eighty-second Street in ten minutes—away from the gayety Honey so eagerly desired, into gloom. She would not let him leave the cab.

"You're tired," she said, "and must hurry home. I'll get in all right. My sister lent me a key. Stay right where you are. Good night."

Honey went heavily up the steps, opened the front door. What a pity he was so slow, so uninteresting. She climbed the two flights of stairs leading to her sister's apartment, taking care not to make any noise. Jane had spoken of a headache in the afternoon; of her desire to go to bed early.

With her latchkey Honey unlocked the door of the apartment, stepped into the tiny front hall. Voices came to her from the living-room —the voices of a woman and a man.

"Jane—you adorable thing!" the man's voice sounded—slow, lazy, caressing. "Don't

"Of course."

With a swift look over her shoulder, Jane stepped back, opening the door wide so that Honey could go in.

"I went to bed very early," she explained, her voice trembling. "You remember, I told you I had a headache."

"Yes."

Honey nodded. She had a heartache herself. Jane, who had preached to her these years, to be carrying on a cheap flirtation! With Don!

"Well," her sister went on, "Mr. Kendall —happened to be passing about ten o'clock, and saw a light in the apartment, so he came in. Waked me out of a sound sleep. You see, I'd asked him to get me a bottle of Scotch sometime, if he could, and he brought it with him. He's here now. Just going, in fact."

She swept aside the curtains and went into the living-room, with Honey at her heels. In the middle of the room stood Don Kendall, fingering his hat. He seemed entirely at ease.

"Hello, Honey," he said. "Mighty glad to see you."

His eyes swept admiringly down the girl's figure, exquisite in her white evening gown— so admiringly, in fact, that Honey blushed.

86 LOVE'S GREATEST MISTAKE

Yet the admiration in his glance did not entirely displease her. There was no denying it, Don Kendall was an attractive man—a very attractive man. Honey remembered that she, too, had once lain helpless in his arms. He had told her, then, that he loved her, just as he had told Jane tonight. Would he ever say that to her again, she wondered—say it and mean it?

CHAPTER XI

"How are you, Don?" Honey said quietly, although she was shaking with excitement.

"Fine." The old charming yet somewhat cynical smile lighted up his eyes, his face. "You are very lovely tonight. Lovely always."

"Thanks!"

Honey forced herself to a coldness she did not entirely feel. There was a caress in his voice which in some subtle way seemed intended for her alone. If she had not seen him, heard him, with Jane a few minutes before, she might almost have believed in him. Now it was impossible—absurd.

"You'll excuse me, won't you?" she murmured. "Good night."

With a contemptuous nod, she hurried down the corridor to her bedroom.

A few minutes later she heard the front door close. Then Jane came to join her.

"Did you find the key?" she asked, throwing

herself on the bed. She was excited, nervous, her breath coming in staccato gasps.

"I haven't looked."

Honey draped the dress she had just taken off over a hanger before she took her purse from the dresser and made a pretense of searching for the key.

"Here it is, after all. Slipped between the lining, just as I thought. If I can ever get at it."

With trembling fingers she tore at the frail silk.

"All right." Jane's voice showed relief from suspicion. "Don't spoil your bag. Funny, Don's stopping in that way—wasn't it? He sometimes does, to smoke a cigarette. I didn't expect him, of course. Had no idea of it. I was sound asleep."

Honey suspected that her sister was not telling the truth, but made no comment.

"Of course," Jane went on, assuming the defensive because Honey said nothing, "it may seem a bit queer to you, my receiving him in this." She indicated her negligee, very delicate and sheer. "But, as I say, I was asleep. And in New York people don't pay so much attention to such things as they do at home.

LOVE'S GREATEST MISTAKE

George would be furious, I suppose, if he knew; but—"

"I won't tell him," Honey said quietly.

"Of course not, dear. It would only make him unhappy—and suspicious. Over nothing —nothing at all. But it isn't George I'm thinking about half as much as it is you."

"Me?" Honey stared. "What have I got to do with it?"

"Nothing, in one way. And yet, in another, perhaps a great deal. You remember, Honey, don't you, that I warned you last night about men like—like this Mr. Ogden you met on the train? And girls like Mona Terry?"

"Yes, I remember. What of it?"

"Well"—Jane rose and began to examine her features in the mirror in order to cover up her embarrassment—"I wouldn't want anything I might do to influence you—set you a bad example: receiving a man alone, at night, in a negligee—anything like that. I'm older than you, child. And I'm married. You have to be careful. If I thought you'd get any queer ideas in your head on account of Don Kendall's being here, I—I'd never forgive myself."

Honey remained silent. There seemed nothing to say. If Jane had known of her pres-

90 LOVE'S GREATEST MISTAKE

ence in the little hall things would have been easier. Oh, well. If people kissed, even married people, it was their own affair, she decided.

"I've said Don is just a friend," Jane went on; "but he—he's more than that, in a way. Honestly, Honey, I believe he cares for me—a little, anyhow." She reddened with confusion as she made the confession. "In a nice way, of course."

Honey thought of the look of admiration Don had just given her, and there seemed something almost pathetic in her sister's faith in that young man. Don, the great lover—the pagan! Jane would never be able to capture him. Honey felt sure of that. Not even if she managed to get rid of George. It would take a cleverer woman—a younger one.

Honey had once indulged in such dreams herself—had dreamed of becoming Mrs. Donald Kendall. She smiled at her conceit. Don had not even troubled to answer the letter she had written him. Perhaps Jane had been the cause of that. Sudden jealousy flamed up in the girl's breast, but she managed to hide it from her sister.

"Have a pleasant evening?" Jane asked.

"Not particularly." Honey's mind was on other matters. "Mr. Gibbs is not my idea of a village cut-up. But he's nice, just the same," she added quickly. "Only serious—terribly serious."

"Just like poor, dear George," Jane said, with a sigh.

When Jane had left her, Honey lay for a long time in the tiny, dark room, thinking. Once more the hum and roar of the city came to her, but it seemed now the roar of a mighty and very cruel wine press, in which thousands of human hearts like her own were being daily crushed to atoms that the wine of Life might be made.

Honey and her sister were just finishing a late breakfast when Jane received a telephone call. From the guarded way in which she spoke, answering in monosyllables, Honey concluded that Don Kendall had called. She was sure of it when Jane announced, a little later, that she was going out, and began to dress with unusual care. She did not ask Honey to go with her.

"I have some shopping to do," she said, "and some business at the bank. If I'm not

92 LOVE'S GREATEST MISTAKE

back for lunch, just get yourself a bite. There's plenty in the ice box."

"All right," Honey smiled. She was greatly pleased by the prospect of having the whole morning to herself.

Opening a newspaper, she began to glance through the Help Wanted advertisements. Rows and rows of them, nearly all calling for experience, references. She possessed neither. The task before her, the prospect of going interminably from office to office looking for a position, suddenly assumed gigantic proportions. She glanced out of the window. The city, by day, seemed a vast gray ant hill, swarming with workers, into whose ranks she would have to fight her way—alone. For a moment her courage wavered.

An advertisement for a cloak model brought Mona Terry to her mind. On impulse she went to the telephone and called her up.

"Can't talk now," Mona said. "I'm busy. Drop in at my apartment this evening. Any time after six. By-by."

Which was that.

Honey had scarcely put down the receiver when the bell tinkled.

LOVE'S GREATEST MISTAKE

"Hello," a guarded voice came over the wire. "Is Mrs. Sommers in?"

"No. She went out about half an hour ago."

Immediately the voice changed, and Honey recognized it.

"Greetings, Honey dear. This is Don. I hoped I'd find you alone."

"Why?" Honey asked coldly, although her heart was pounding.

"You certainly did look wonderful last night, darlin'," the voice went on, ignoring her question. "I couldn't keep my eyes off you. Say, Honey, I've got to see you."

"What about?" Honey said, even more coldly. She could not help remembering the scene of the night before.

"Can't explain over the telephone, but it's important. How about meeting me in the lobby of the Vanderbilt? Around five."

An impulse to refuse point blank rose in Honey's mind, but something checked it. Don certainly owed her explanations—why not allow him to make them?

"Very well," she said quietly. "But I can't stay. I have an engagement at six."

She hung up the receiver, patches of scarlet in her cheeks.

She had just finished a late luncheon when a telegram came for her. It was from New Haven:

> LEAVING HERE ON TRAIN ARRIVING GRAND CENTRAL FOUR-THIRTY. IF POSSIBLE MEET ME FOR TEA. HERBERT GIBBS.

Honey stared at the telegram, a frown of perplexity in her eyes. Since there was no way in which she could communicate with Mr. Gibbs, only two courses lay open to her. One was to meet him, as he asked, and explain her previous engagement. The other, to ignore his wire completely. But Herbert Gibbs was, after all, a pleasant friend. She would have a few minutes with him, at least.

"I must be getting popular," she laughed. "Three engagements in one afternoon. I guess I'll wear my gray crêpe."

Honey had made the frock herself, from an alleged Paris model in a woman's magazine. But she was too lovely to look other than charming in whatever she wore.

She was at the station too early, but Mr. Gibbs' pleasure at seeing her made amends for her wait. Honey, as she saw him coming toward her, thought him, for the first time, almost good looking. It surprised her, too, to realize how muscular and well built he was. He had new color in his cheeks, a new brightness in his eyes. He did not seem at all the studious person she had pictured him.

"Hello," he said. "It certainly was sweet of you to meet me. Where shall we go for tea?"

"I'm afraid we can't go anywhere," Honey told him. "I have another engagement—at five." Then, as she saw his disappointment: "I'm awfully sorry. There wasn't any way to let you know."

Mr. Gibbs glanced ruefully at his watch.

"I never was lucky," he grinned. "Perhaps another day. It's twenty minutes to five now. Have you far to go?"

"The Vanderbilt," Honey said. "Is that far?"

"No. Only a few blocks. Suppose we have a—a soda instead of tea. Pretty dusty ride down. I'm thirsty."

At the soda counter, they talked about Honey's efforts to find work.

"How's everything going?" Herbert asked.

"I've made a list from the newspapers," she said. "Hope I shan't have to go back home.

a failure." She gave him one of her brilliant smiles. "It isn't nice to admit that you have failed."

Mr. Gibbs greeted this remark with a gay laugh.

"You—fail?" he said. "Impossible. Do you know, Honey, your mission in life is to make some man a wonderful wife—not to spend your days over a typewriter."

"Really? That sounds fine. But I've got to live, you know, while I'm looking for a man."

"Do you think he would be very hard to find?"

"Well—nobody has offered to pay my board and lodging yet. There are lots of attractive women in New York. Millions. I'm just a very small frog in a perfectly enormous ocean. Nobody knows I exist."

"That isn't fair." Herbert gazed down at her, his expression suddenly very tender. "I know it—and appreciate it—tremendously. There are mighty few women in New York as attractive as you are. At least, none that I know. You're—wonderful!"

Honey glanced at the clock.

"Ten minutes to five," she said.

"Plenty of time," Mr. Gibbs grumbled. "I'll take you down in a cab."

He was annoyed, and Honey saw it. When they were seated in the taxi, she bent toward him, lovely, vital, fragrant.

"I wonder if you'd let me call you Herbert," she whispered. "You call me Honey, you know."

"Try it," he whispered back. "Just try it."

"Herbert," she dared, smiling.

Then Herbert Gibbs swept her into his arms and gave her a swift, eager kiss. He was somewhat clumsy about it, and crushed her hat a little. By the time she had arranged it they had arrived at the hotel.

"I'm sorry," he said.

Was he thinking of the hat?

"Don't be. It—it's quite all right. Call me up sometime."

With gay lights in her eyes, she sprang out of the cab and ran up the steps of the hotel.

CHAPTER XII

BEFORE Don caught sight of Honey she saw him, towering above the throng like some ruddy young giant. He was staring out over the heads of the crowd, his chin lifted, his mouth hard drawn. Seeing him thus, it was easy to picture him driving hawklike through the air, to strike down some unwary opponent. For an instant Honey's heart trembled. Perhaps he was waiting to strike her down, as he had others! Swiftly, ruthlessly—even carelessly.

Suddenly he caught sight of her and came forward, his hand outstretched, his face wearing the old familiar smile.

"My, it's good to see you, dear," he said, drawing Honey to a seat beside him. "Seems like ages, almost, doesn't it?"

In spite of the thrill she always felt in his presence, Honey refused to smile.

"It does seem like ages since you've paid any attention to me. And you never even answered my letter."

"There was a reason for that."

"What reason?"

"Your sister asked me, the day after the party at Ben Troup's, to let you alone; not to see you. She said you were just a—kid, and that people at home would talk if I went around with you so much."

"But—why—if you—if you meant it?"

"Oh—because of my reputation, I suppose. Nobody thinks I'm in earnest. A bad egg. You know how it is when a fellow has a little money. They say he's just—amusing himself. I guess that was right, too, in a way. So, when she asked me to lay off—"

"You decided to amuse yourself with her," Honey interrupted bitterly.

"Well—why not? She's a very charming, very beautiful woman. Bored with life. If it has pleased her to be taken to a few parties, what's the harm? There's been nothing wrong about it. Dancing—some drinks! Good Lord! A fellow must have some fun in life."

"It may be fun to you," Honey retorted, still refusing to respond to his smile; "but it won't be for Jane if she keeps on thinking you care for her."

"What makes you say that? Does she think I care for her?"

"I'm afraid she does."

"Well, I do—in a way. She's bright, amusing, cheers a fellow up. And tremendously good looking. But I've never cared for her the way I do for you."

Honey thought of the scene she had witnessed the night before. Was Don a liar? Or did he really like her as much as he said?

"That night at Ben Troup's," he went on, his voice heavy with caresses, "I told you I loved you. I still do. I want to see you—to be with you. That's why I telephoned this morning. I want you to have dinner with me sometime—very soon. Did you say you had an engagement tonight?"

"Yes."

"So have I. Some friends have asked me to go to the Paradise Club. But I simply had to see you, after last night. Call me up, dear, in the morning. But don't let Jane know. She thinks I'm some terrible wolf, ready to devour her beautiful little sister. And I'm nothing of the sort. Just a man who admires you very much. You are beautiful, Honey dear. Very

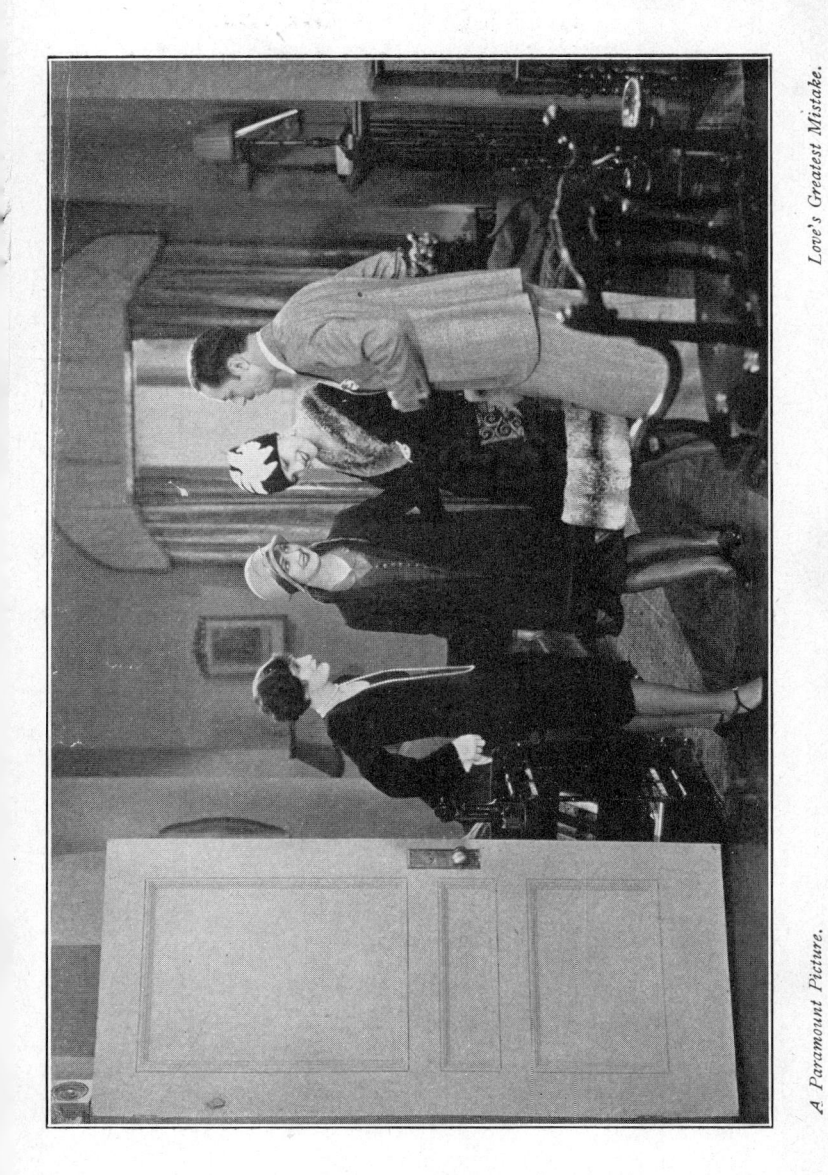

A Paramount Picture. HONEY IS INTRODUCED TO JANE'S FAST NEW YORK SET. *Love's Greatest Mistake.*

beautiful. Any man might be proud just to be seen with you. So sweet!" He pressed her fingers in his big, powerful ones until Honey winced. "You believe me, don't you?"

"I don't know," she gasped, realizing that she felt something, whenever she was with him, that she felt in the presence of no other man— some tremendous attraction that seemed always to be sweeping her into his arms. Weakness, perhaps. She felt glad that they were in a hotel lobby.

With an abruptness characteristic of all his motions, he suddenly rose.

"Sorry, dear, that I must run along. Just time to dress for dinner. It's been wonderful, our having even these few minutes together. You will call me up, won't you? May I drop you anywhere? My car's outside."

"No," Honey whispered, faint, confused. "I'm not going far." Mona Terry's apartment on Madison Avenue was just a few blocks away. For a moment she clung almost desperately to his hand, then dropped it. "Goodby."

Honey sat in the lobby for many minutes, keenly aware of the spell Don had cast about her—of her pounding heart. After a time she got up, almost wearily, and went out to the noisy street.

Mona Terry was dressing for dinner when Honey arrived at her apartment. She opened the door, wearing the filmiest of step-ins.

"Welcome, little stranger," she exclaimed. "I'm just getting into my make-up. Come along."

She dashed through the studio living-room into the bedroom adjoining, and resumed her seat before a triple-mirrored dressing-table.

"Cigarettes over there. No cocktails till my boy friend gets here with the liquor. Can't keep the stuff overnight these days."

She applied some final touches of mascara to her lashes, swung around on her stool.

"Glad to see you, Honey child. You're the first person from the old home town ever took the trouble to look me up."

"What a beautiful apartment you have!" Honey exclaimed, dazzled by the array of furniture, hangings, rugs. "Simply lovely. And you're lovely yourself."

"Think so?" Mona laughed. "Well, my boy friend says I'm the Queen of Sheba to him. So that's all right." She gave Honey a long, critical stare. "Say, kid, you're not hard to look at yourself—even in that bunch of rags you're wearing. In the right clothes you'd be a knockout."

She slipped into a fluffy evening gown of green chiffon. Against it her red hair flamed like a torch.

"How's Sally? Still talking her fool head off? Some head—for a pin. If she'd break loose—come to New York, the way you have—I'd make something of her. Found anything to do yet?"

"No." Honey shook her head. "I don't know anybody—not anybody I can go to. There was a man I met on the train—"

"Money?" Mona asked quickly.

"Yes. Plenty of it, I guess. And awfully nice."

She explained in detail her little experience with Mr. Ogden.

"Go to it, kid. If you make him run after you hard enough, you're certain to catch him. Men are mostly alike. Use all the good looks God gave you and keep them guessing. That's my system. And don't let them fool you with promises, either. Get it in writing—certified checks. I'd look this bozo up if I were you. But dress the part, first. Nothing like a good

104 LOVE'S GREATEST MISTAKE

front to get the money. They put them on banks, don't they?"

Mona ran a comb swiftly through her bobbed hair.

"Wish that boy friend of mine would hurry. Say"—she paused in the act of lighting a cigarette—"why not make it a party of four? He can get a man for you."

"I'm not dressed," Honey objected.

"I can fix you up. Look here." She threw open the door of a closet in which a row of gowns hung from a brass rod. "Help yourself. I'd like to see you really dolled up once. I bet you'd hand us all a surprise."

Honey began to laugh. Always, it seemed, she was destined to appear in borrowed finery. Would she never have any lovely things of her own? Somehow, the question turned her thoughts to Mr. William Ogden; but Mona quickly turned them back again.

"Here," she said, dragging a fragile evening gown from one of the hangers. "This ought to suit you. One of our newest models. Flowered chiffon. I get these things from the shop—at a discount, of course."

Mona pulled stockings from a drawer, satin slippers from their trees in the closet. "Put

LOVE'S GREATEST MISTAKE 105

these things on while I give my sweetie a buzz and tell him to bring a friend. Then I'll come back and hand you a few points about make-up. I see you don't know anything about it."

Mona's friend, Mr. Ray Becker, presently arrived, bringing with him his roommate, Mr. Eddie Morse. When they had been introduced, Mr. Morse, after one glance at Honey, struck an impressive attitude, made a sweeping gesture.

"A successor to Mary Pickford at last!" he exclaimed. "And I don't mean maybe, either. Mona, where have you been hiding this dream of beauty? She's a wow! A knockout! The screen's just been waiting for her."

"Friend of mine," Miss Terry remarked dryly. "Run along into the bathroom and help Ray with those cocktails. We're late, as it is. What did you have to do—make this gin?"

"Eddie's in good form tonight," she went on to Honey, when the two men had gone. "He does something over at the United Studios. Gag man, I believe. Good egg to know, if you're thinking of going into pictures. But don't fall for that line of his about making you a star overnight because you're so beautiful. It's old stuff. Just string him along and promise him nothing. He only makes about three hundred a week, and that's just cigarette money in New York. And, by the way, kid, I don't know anything about your capacity, but if you're not in the habit of drinking this homemade gin, watch your step. You drink half a dozen rounds of cocktails, and then something creeps up on you and crowns you with a piece of lead pipe. Get me?''

Honey nodded as the two men returned to the room, one with a cocktail shaker, the other bearing glasses. Mr. Becker, whom she judged to be under thirty, was slim and dark, and extremely well dressed. He gave a curious impression of sleekness, from his shining black hair to his equally shining shoes. A smooth sleekness. His smile was quick and disarming, but there was a glint of something raw and cold in his rather small dark eyes.

Mr. Morse, his companion, was not at all good-looking, but Honey liked him better. There was quick humor in his homely face and laughter in his eyes. Just a good-natured boy, she thought, slipping her second cocktail behind some books on the table.

Mona was arguing with Ray Becker over the question of a place to dine. After each of sev-

LOVE'S GREATEST MISTAKE 107

eral suggestions Mr. Becker shook his head and Honey heard him say, "Padlocked."

"Isn't there a place called the Paradise, or something like that?" she asked rather timidly.

The others stared at her.

"Sure. The very place!" Mr. Morse exclaimed. "A lot of picture people go there. I'd like some of them to see this kid. Myself, I think she's the coming queen of the movies."

"What made you think of the Paradise Club?" Mona asked Honey. "It's one of the niftiest joints in town. And you only in New York a couple of days!"

"I—I've heard about it," Honey stammered. "A friend of mine spoke of dining there."

"Not this bird William Ogden you met on the train," Mona laughed—"the one who was so crazy about you?"

At mention of Mr. Ogden's name Mr. Becker's small eyes showed curious glints.

"Do you mean William Ogden, the banker?" he asked softly. "In the Union Trust Building?"

"I believe that is his address," Honey replied, confused. "But he's not the one I was speaking of."

Mr. Becker gave Mona a slow stare. His hand moved almost imperceptibly in the direction of the bedroom.

"Excuse us a moment, folks, won't you?" he said gayly. "Mona's got a little matter on her mind she wants to talk to me about."

The two went into the next room, closing the door.

When they were alone, Becker turned to his companion and spoke in a voice as brittle as tempered steel, yet so low that it could scarcely be heard a yard away.

"Ogden's worth forty million," he whispered. "With an invalid wife. What could be sweeter? Do I understand he picked this girl up on a train and tried to make a date with her?"

"So she tells me."

"All right. Stick close to her—see? Get her under your thumb. Keep her there till I'm ready. Don't let Eddie Morse or anyone else turn her head. Ogden's a fox. Nobody has been able to land him—yet. But they all fall, sooner or later, if the trap's baited right. This girl's a queen for looks. And innocent as a two-year-old. She doesn't know what it's all about. Ogden realized that. You do as I tell

LOVE'S GREATEST MISTAKE 109

you and we'll frame this bird for some real jack. I'll figure out the details tonight."

Mona stared and stared, her eyes narrowing.

"Honey's a friend of mine."

"Friend, eh?" Mr. Becker's voice was as smooth as his oiled hair, but his eyes were black flint. "What am I, then? The office boy? The boob who pays the rent?" He took a step forward, grasped Mona by the wrist. "You do what I tell you, you poor piece of cheese, or I'll break every bone in your body. Play that on your piano."

CHAPTER XIII

Honey glanced with frank curiosity around the brilliant night club to which Mona Terry, Ray Becker, and Eddie Morse had brought her. Don Kendall, she thought, was probably somewhere within this perfumed, music-laden place.

In that atmosphere of artificiality, of sophistication, Honey seemed a rose with the dew on it, surrounded by wax imitations. She did not notice the admiring glances of the men at near-by tables, because she was thinking of Don. Romance—and Don. Her eyes sought for him everywhere.

Across the table, Ray Becker was talking to Mona Terry in close-clipped undertones, almost without moving his lips.

Eddie Morse began to relate a wordy story.

The yarn fell flat as far as Honey was concerned; for suddenly she saw Don Kendall, moving out on the dance floor, a woman in his arms—a lovely, dark creature with petulant lips and an insolent stare.

As he caught sight of Honey in her borrowed

LOVE'S GREATEST MISTAKE

finery, Don almost stopped in his tracks. This was not the Honey he had known. He stared incredulously.

Ten minutes later he was at their table, gay, smiling, debonair.

"Honey darlin'," he whispered, leaning over her chair, "you're wonderful! Simply wonderful! I'm mad about you. Honestly."

"I suppose you just told that charming brunette the same thing," she laughed.

"Not exactly. She's married to one of my best friends."

"Would that make any difference to *you?*"

"Not a bit, if I loved her," Don replied. "Nothing would. Are you going to give me a dance later on?"

"Certainly, if your married lady will let you off long enough."

"I'll see to it." He flashed a smile and was gone.

"You say his name is Kendall?" Ray Becker asked, other questions forming in his chilly eyes.

"Yes. A boy from my home town. His father is president of a big steamship company here in New York."

"I see." Mr. Becker made mental notes.

"Nice-looking chap. How about another drink?"

"I can dance, too, you know, baby doll," Mr. Morse announced, rising. He whirled Honey out on the floor. "Is the handsome young sheik with the hot eyes the hero of the piece?" he grinned.

"There isn't any hero yet," Honey flashed back. "And I doubt if my sheik looks me up again."

An hour later, however, Honey found herself once more in Don Kendall's arms. How superbly he danced!

"You're so sweet," he whispered, straining her to him. "So terribly sweet. No wonder they call you Honey. Do you remember that night?"

"When you first told me you loved me?" Honey laughed, but her lips were trembling.

"Yes. You know I care. And shall—always. When am I going to see you again?"

"I don't know. I'll call you up—maybe."

He was holding her so close that she could scarcely breathe. The thought of him crushing Jane in his arms, declaring his love for *her*, the night before, swept through Honey's brain, stabbing cruelly.

LOVE'S GREATEST MISTAKE 113

"Can't we sit down somewhere—for a moment?" she gasped.

"Why, of course."

He whirled her into the lounge, drew her to a soft-cushioned divan.

"What's wrong, dear?" The pressure of his fingers on her arm hurt her.

"Last night"—Honey steeled herself to speak the accusing words—"when I came home after dining with Mr. Gibbs, I—I opened the door of my sister's apartment—with a latch-key, and saw you holding her in your arms—kissing her—telling her—" Sobs prevented her from going on.

Don's face was a mask. Would he try to explain away that scene?

"You were spying on me, then—you of all people," Don Kendall exclaimed. "Good God!"

"You know better than that, Don," Honey cried. "I came in quietly, thinking Jane was asleep—not supposing anyone was there. I went out again, so as not to embarrass you—and her. But, after hearing what I did, how can I—how can you—" Again she broke down.

Don's face was a mask. Only his eyes showed the storm that was raging within him.

"All right," he muttered. "I told you I was a rotten—a bad egg. I'm sorry you had to find it out the way you did, but I suppose you would have sooner or later, anyhow. Only, people—people like me, I guess—do things sometimes on impulse—silly things—that mean nothing—really.

"I don't expect you to believe in me. I don't expect you to believe in anything. Why should you? A girl's a fool who does. Let's go back to the table."

He stalked off, his chin lifted, his face wearing the expression that always made Honey think of a hawk about to swoop on its prey.

She felt confused, baffled. Why should he show such bitterness, such anger? Was he angry with her? Or with himself? Or both?

Just then, through a mist of suffering, she pictured him as she had seen him an hour before, as he moved out on the dance floor, a woman in his arms—a lovely dark creature, with petulant lips and an insolent stare.

Wearily she dropped into the chair at her table, thankful that Ray and Mona were dancing—that only Mr. Morse was left to witness her confusion.

"I'm sorry, Don," she whispered up at him.

But Don Kendall's anger had not left him. With a cool, almost impersonal "Good night," he was gone.

Honey watched him as he crossed the floor, head and shoulders above the crowd. Only when Eddie Morse had spoken to her for the third time, asking her if she wanted to dance, did she hear him.

"No." She shook her head, struggling to collect her thoughts. "I—I'm a little tired."

"Did the big boy try to get rough with you?" Mr. Morse asked.

"Of course not."

Honey forced a smile. Why, after all, should she worry about Don—permit him to spoil her evening? There was nothing sincere about him. His anger came from the knowledge that he had been found out. She even managed to laugh as she saw Mona and Ray Becker coming toward the table.

"Let's go," the latter said, calling for his check.

"Where to?" Mona was still in an evil temper.

"Tony Briggs, the press agent," remarked Mr. Morse, "is giving a party at his studio in the Alcazar tonight. Asked me to bring along

116 LOVE'S GREATEST MISTAKE

my friends. We might look in there for a while."

"I was thinking of the Red Peacock," said Mona.

"No." Mr. Becker frowned on the suggestion. "I don't think Honey would care for that night-club crowd—at least, not yet awhile. Later on, maybe, when she's learned her way about."

Honey saw nothing unusual in the remark; but Mr. Morse gave Ray a quick stare, while Mona's full lips curled in a cynical smile.

Mr. Becker paid the check and rose. As they went out, he dropped back a space, drew Mona to him.

"We don't want this kid to know too much when she meets Ogden," he whispered. "She's got to tell him she's never seen a night club before. When she goes to one, let *him* take her. And you want to work quick, before she gets mixed up with that Kendall fellow. He's got her pretty near where he wants her, right now."

Mona's only reply was a sullen nod, whereupon Mr. Becker regarded her with snarling contempt.

"A hell of a pal you are," he muttered.

LOVE'S GREATEST MISTAKE

"Don't try to pull that sob-sister stuff on me. Keep your mind on the race."

Honey, knowing nothing of the web that was being woven around her, moved through the next few hours on the wings of youth. If she thought of Don, it was subconsciously. She did her best to put him out of her mind.

Mr. Morse, as they drove uptown, told her something of the beauties of Mr. Briggs' studio, but the reality far exceeded Honey's expectations.

The great, two-storied room, with its tapestries, its Chinese rugs, its tall lamps, made a brilliant picture of light and shade, glowing color and deep shadow, crimson and orange against purple darkness. White arms and shoulders beneath eager painted faces. A radio playing. Some couples dancing. Others hovering near a long Italian table littered with food. Champagne bubbling pleasantly in wide-mouthed glasses. Honey had never tasted it until now. Men—many men—being presented to her, whose names she did not remember, whose faces she forgot a moment later.

Mona and Ray Becker were always at her elbow, the one still sulking rebelliously, the other smooth, sleek, watchful, seeing everything, taking care that no one held her long in conversation. This Honey did not particularly mind, being in no mood for the obvious love-making everywhere thrust upon her.

They left her at the apartment door at half-past one, Mona promising to do something at once about finding her a position.

Jane, whom she found sitting up, seemed unduly anxious.

"I've been worried about you, Honey," she said. "You oughtn't to stay out so late—especially with that Terry girl. She'll get you into trouble, mark my words."

Honey was in no mood for a lecture.

"It isn't late," she yawned. "And you're all wrong about Mona Terry. She's the only person, so far, who has tried to help me. Good night. I'm sleepy."

About meeting Don Kendall at the Paradise Club she mentioned nothing at all to Jane.

CHAPTER XIV

Honey had intended to spend the next day in a round of visits to business offices, in the hope of finding a position; but her plans were upset by a telephone call from Mona Terry immediately after breakfast.

"Hello—this you, Honey?" the latter began in a high, bright voice. "Listen. You remember I promised last night to do what I could about finding you a job. Well—I've got a great idea—see? And I want to talk it over with you. Meet me in front of the shop at twelve, will you? Don't be late. I'm taking a couple of hours off on your account."

Honey, who had been searching the Help Wanted columns of the newspapers for hours, was immensely pleased—flattered. But even in her excitement she noticed that Jane seemed greatly depressed.

"Have you heard from Mr. Kendall lately?" Honey asked, watching her sister's face.

"No. I've been expecting him to telephone

all the morning. I think he must be out of town."

Don was not out of town, and Honey knew it. During their little talk at the Vanderbilt the afternoon before he had extracted from Honey a promise to call him up, with the idea of their dining together. Had he determined to break with Jane in order to prove to Honey that he really cared for *her?*

It would be like him, Honey thought. He could be cruel—very cruel. Somehow, she did not dislike him for that quality. At least, he was no weakling. A strong man. A ruthless man. The sort of man women love. In spite of her anger, Honey's heart still beat faster whenever she thought of him. And, in spite of their quarrel the evening before, in spite of the almost brutal way in which he had left her, Honey still found herself wondering when she would see him again.

When she began to dress to go out she remembered the evening gown Mona had lent her —remembered, too, that her prized gray crêpe, her best shoes and stockings, had been left at Mona's apartment. Well, she reflected, her second best would have to do—her striped broadcloth. Jane had said it looked like an awning, but Mona wouldn't mind. She wrapped up the latter's evening gown very neatly and carefully, to take along with her.

Just as she was ready to leave, a boy arrived with a box of flowers for her. Honey's fingers trembled as she opened it, Jane at her side. Suppose Don had sent them! It would mean explanations—a scene, perhaps. She lifted the big bunches of white and red roses from the box, and asked Jane to put them in water, while she glanced at the card. Her fears were groundless. The flowers came from Herbert Gibbs, with a little note. Honey read it aloud:

I am sending you white and red roses because I thing you are like both.

"Herbert's nice," she said, rather pleased that he did not think her all snow and ice. Perhaps their kiss in the taxicab had told him something, had caused him to send red roses along with the white ones—pure white and passion red. She tucked the card into her purse, and asked Jane to say, should he call up, that she would certainly be back by 5 o'clock.

"I do hope Mona can help me find something to do," she told Jane, as she went out.

122 LOVE'S GREATEST MISTAKE

"Mother gave me fifty dollars when I came away; but, what with my railroad ticket and all, it's nearly half gone now."

"Yes," Jane said slowly. "You'll be better off with something to do."

Mona, who was waiting for her in front of the little shop, darted in to leave her evening gown. In a moment she was back again, waving toward a passing cab.

"First we'll have lunch and talk," she announced, when she and Honey were seated. "Then we have some shopping to do."

Honey wondered what the shopping might be, but did not ask. She would wait, she concluded, until Mona had explained the object of their meeting, which Miss Terry did, very suavely, over a luncheon of chicken croquettes and asparagus.

"You came to New York to find work, didn't you?" she asked. "Right. Well, running around nights, going to parties, all that, isn't going to get you anywhere. Now listen to me. This man Ogden, the one you met on the train, offered to give you a job, didn't he?"

"Why—yes—in a way. He said he would see what he could do. And gave me this."

Honey took from her purse the card **Mr.**

Ogden had given her and handed it to Mona.

"There's something written on the back."

Mona's eyes narrowed as she read the penciled words:

Admit Miss McNeill at any time. W. O.

"I see. Well, dear, I asked Ray to look him up—on your account. Ray has a great many friends in the financial district. He finds that Mr. Ogden is an important man; nice in every way; generous to a fault. He evidently took a fancy to you or he wouldn't have given you this."

She glanced down at the card.

"Men like him are almost impossible to reach, ordinarily. Of course he saw at once that you were a decent kid, not a gold-digger. You are very foolish, Ray says, not to go to him at once, before he forgets you, and try for a position. These young fellows like Mr. Kendall won't help you any. And tramping from office to office looking for work is—hell. I've tried it and I know. Take my advice and see Mr. Ogden—this afternoon. He isn't the sort of man to try to put anything over on you. A gentleman all through, Ray says. *I* think it's a wonderful chance, myself."

124 LOVE'S GREATEST MISTAKE

"I guess you're right," Honey said slowly. "Anyway, it can't do any harm to try."

"Of course you mustn't see him in that nightmare you're wearing. You've got to look fresh—smart. Have some charm. And make use of it. Let him feel that you're a young and beautiful woman. We're going out now to get you something fit to wear."

"No use," Honey laughed. "I couldn't pay for it."

"That's all right. I'm going to lend you the money."

"But—why?"

Honey's eyes grew big as she saw her friend take three $100 bills from her purse.

"Because I like you—that's why. I've got a little jack saved up. You can pay me back, so much a week, when you land a job."

Mona's gray-green eyes flashed kindly interest. Honey did not notice the ugly purple bruises on her forearm.

"I saw a little two-piece frock on the Avenue the other day that would just suit you. Mauve, with white collar and cuffs. Some new material. Very simple, very sweet. With the right stockings, shoes, hat, I'll have you looking like a million dollars."

"But," Honey objected, "I don't want to look like a million dollars when I ask Mr. Ogden for work."

Mona laughed, a loud, full laugh.

"You won't—to him," she said. "A woman might realize what you had on, but a man— never. The general effect is all Mr. Ogden will see, and that effect is going to be the very simple little-girl effect for which middle-aged gentlemen like Mr. Ogden always fall the hardest."

William Ogden, as unaware as was Honey of the web fate was weaving around them, sat in his office that afternoon signing some letters. A long conference with his attorneys at luncheon had left him a trifle tired—perhaps even a trifle bored.

Mr. Ogden was more than a successful business man. Money-making had never entirely absorbed his energies. He was interested in many things, from Japanese prints to race horses. And since beauty, in any form, appealed vividly to the artistic side of his nature, he loved beautiful women—with a real, æsthetic appreciation of things finer, rarer, different. In short, he was a connoisseur.

He had just finished reading the last of the

letters when his secretary came in, bearing a card.

Mr. Ogden took it, a puzzled expression upon his face.

"The young woman is waiting outside," the secretary said.

Mr. Ogden read the message on the card—reread it. Then recollection came. The little girl on the train, whom he had taken to luncheon. There had been something striking, something unusual, about her; but he could not remember now what it was. He regretted having given the card, but it was necessary to redeem the promise he had written upon it.

"Show her in," he said.

Honey came timidly through the open doorway.

Mona had done her part extremely well. The little frock with its white collar and cuffs, the untrimmed but expensive felt hat, the low-heeled walking shoes, the almost complete absence of make-up, presented to Mr. Ogden's eyes a picture of simplicity that was perfect. Honey's unusual beauty had never been shown to better advantage.

"I came," she whispered, "because—because you said—"

LOVE'S GREATEST MISTAKE 127

"Yes," Mr. Ogden smiled, waving toward a chair. "What did I say—Honey? You told me, didn't you, that everyone called you that?"

Honey smiled too, then. She did not feel timid any longer.

"You said, Mr. Ogden, that if I came here you might be able to help me find work—"

"Let me see. Just what kind of work was it? Typing?"

"Yes. I know how to use a machine. Pretty well, anyway. I'm sure all I need is practice."

Mr. Ogden laughed. Not for twenty years had he personally engaged a typist. It made him feel young again.

"What salary do you expect—Honey?" he asked, after a pause.

"Why, Mr. Ogden, I—I'd be willing to leave that entirely to you," Honey assured him. "In the beginning, of course, I'd take 'most anything to get a start."

Mr. Ogden pressed a button, whereupon his secretary appeared automatically.

"Please ask Mr. Roder to step in here."

While they were waiting, he examined Honey's rose-and-white beauty critically.

"Has your sister shown you all the sights of the town?" he asked.

128 LOVE'S GREATEST MISTAKE

"No, Mr. Ogden, not yet. But, from what I've seen, I think New York the most wonderful place!"

There was a breathless quality in her enthusiasm which immediately caused Mr. Ogden to think that it might be a very pleasant thing to show New York and its wonders to anyone so unspoiled.

"Yes, child," he said gravely. "Wonderful and—dangerous. Be careful whom you trust. The jungle is full of wild beasts, you know, although you might often fail to recognize them in everyday clothes. Ah—Roder"—he addressed an elderly spectacled man who came into the room—"this young woman, a friend of some friends of mine, is looking for employment. As a typist, I believe. If you can make use of her—" He paused significantly.

"Miss Watson is leaving to be married, sir, on the first."

"Yes? I did not know. Use your own judgment, Roder. If Miss McNeill can do the work—"

Again he paused, and Honey rose.

"Thank you for the chance, Mr. Ogden," she said quietly. "Good day."

With her heart pounding, she followed Mr. Roder into the outer office.

CHAPTER XV

THE first result of Honey's visit to Mr. Ogden's office was that she received a position there, at a salary of twenty-five dollars a week. She spent her days very agreeably, from nine in the morning until five in the afternoon, copying business documents of various sorts on the typewriter.

Being careful in her work, precise, if a trifle slow, she earned Mr. Roder's praise, which was something of an achievement.

The comments made by those interested in her progress were various. Mr. Becker, for instance, remarked to Mona Terry:

"It's a good start. All we have to do now is let nature take its course."

Whereupon Mona, with a sulky look, had replied:

"I've never been strong for this thing, Ray, from the start, and I wouldn't be in it now if I weren't fool enough to be crazy about you."

"If you don't like it, you know the answer," Ray said, reaching for his hat; at which

Mona's timid rebellion ended in tears.

Jane was extremely practical.

"You may stay on here for the present, Honey," she said, "and pay me a nominal board—say, twelve dollars a week. That will leave you thirteen for spending money."

"Not quite," Honey sighed. "I have to pay Mona Terry five a week on account of those clothes she bought me. I'll have only eight, for carfare and lunches and everything."

Herbert Gibbs, whom Honey saw a day or two later, admitted that, if Honey had to go to work, she was lucky to find it in such an office as Mr. Ogden's.

"A fine man, they say. Our firm designed his house in Southampton. It cost a quarter of a million. Mrs. Ogden, I believe, has something the matter with her heart. Her husband's a great collector. Do you see anything of him?"

"Not much," Honey replied. "He's called me in, once or twice, about changes in papers I was copying. Asked me how I was getting along. *I* think he's a peach. And awfully good-looking. You'd never suppose he was fifty."

Herbert frowned. He and Honey were lunching together—something not difficult, since their offices were less than a dozen blocks apart.

"I'd be careful of friendly millionaires," he announced jealously; "especially good-looking ones."

His tone made Honey suddenly angry.

"What do you mean?" she flared. "Mr. Ogden is a gentleman."

"I haven't questioned that."

"You—you've implied—other things."

"Have I? Well—you're a very attractive girl, my dear. Any man can see that—even a millionaire of fifty with an invalid wife. Suppose he should try to make love to you?"

"It takes two—for that," Honey retorted. "Do you mean to suggest that I—" She was pink with rage, and Herbert made profuse apologies. Honey accepted them; but her annoyance remained, and they did not see each other again for a week. Her proposed visit to Stamford, to meet his mother and sisters, had been delayed by the absence of Mrs. Gibbs, who was visiting in Boston. As for Herbert, work on the drawings for the competition in Washington occupied all his spare time.

Don had not telephoned since the night of their quarrel at the Paradise Club—neither to

Honey nor to Jane. But Honey had received a brief and characteristic note from him—received and opened it under Jane's very nose, just as she was leaving for the office:

Am going out of town for a couple of weeks [Don wrote]. When I get back I want to see you.

That was all. The address on the envelope had been typewritten. Honey knew, from Jane's increasing depression, that her sister had not heard from Don and was worrying because of it. Rather cruel and cold-blooded way to treat anyone, she thought, and resented it—on Jane's account.

Then it came to her that the whole matter was rather stupid and silly. Why should either she or Jane allow herself to be worried, upset, by a man like Don Kendall? A reckless war bird, who lived only for his own selfish pleasures. Attractive, certainly, but worthless. A killer of men—and of women.

She tore his note into shreds, tossed them into the gutter. Deliberately—significantly. She was through with him, forever. A new gayety entered her heart.

That night, when she left the office, it was

A Paramount Picture.   *Love's Greatest Mistake.*
HARVEY IS WORRIED AS FLOWERS ARRIVE FROM THE MILLIONAIRE OGDEN.

raining hard; and, since the morning had been clear, she had neither raincoat nor umbrella. As she stood in the entrance of the building, hoping the shower would pass, a man in livery, a chauffeur, came up to her, carrying an open umbrella.

"Mr. Ogden says if you will step around to his car, miss," the man told her, "he will drive you uptown."

For a moment Honey hesitated. Then she thought of the absurdity of refusing so pleasant an offer. Even Jane, who claimed the right to preach to her, had accepted gifts from Don Kendall—Scotch whisky, if nothing more. And Mona, cynical Mona, had advised her to be nice to Mr. Ogden in a decent, friendly way. What better opportunity, than to drive uptown in his car? And, in addition, it would avoid ruining her hat and frock. With a nod, she joined the man, walking beneath his umbrella to the corner. A limousine stood along the curb. When Honey stepped in, Mr. Ogden helped her to a seat.

"I was kept late by a directors' meeting," he said, smiling. "Where may I take you?"

"To Eighty-second Street, if it isn't out of your way."

134 LOVE'S GREATEST MISTAKE

Honey gave her sister's address, and Mr. Ogden repeated it to his chauffeur.

"Not a bit. I'm only too glad to have company—such charming company, too. How do you like it at the office?"

"I think it's wonderful. Mr. Roder has been so kind—and you."

"Don't thank me. Roder's a practical man. If your work hadn't been good he would not have kept you. I leave all such matters to him."

They fell into conversation, then, about Honey and her affairs, Mr. Ogden questioning her closely while apologizing for his frankness.

"I'm really interested," he said, with his pleasant smile. "It's a mystery to me how a girl can get along on twenty-five dollars a week and dress as smartly as you do."

"Well," Honey smiled back, "I live at my sister's for one thing. Pay her board, of course—twelve dollars. As for my clothes, I make most of them. But this frock I'm wearing I bought, on the installment plan—five dollars a week. So just now I have only eight left for carfare and lunches and—oh, all sorts of things a girl needs!"

She was so delightfully simple, so real, that

Mr. Ogden was delighted and made a mental note to have Roder raise her salary. First, however, he decided to test her in another way.

"Money means very little to me," he said. "I give a great deal away. Now, if you will let me pay for that dress—"

"Couldn't think of it!" Honey laughed back at him. " 'Rags are royal raiment,' you know. I'll get along. But I thank you, just the same."

Mr. Ogden was charmed. This girl was certainly very different from most of those one met. He tried another tack.

"Speaking of amusements," he said, "I suppose you have friends—men friends—who take you out evenings?"

"Only two. One is Herbert Gibbs, a young architect. He's working on a competition nights, so he goes out very little. The other, a boy named Kendall, is from my home town. He's asked me once or twice, but I haven't gone yet. Of course, I'm just dying to see the restaurants and supper clubs you hear so much about. I suppose any girl from a small town would feel that way. And I love to dance. When Don comes back—"

"You're not engaged to him, by any chance, are you?" Mr. Ogden asked quickly.

"Heavens, no! I'm not engaged to anyone. Not even in love."

"And you want to go to a night club? You must promise to let me take you. Not that I often visit such places, but I see no reason why we shouldn't join forces in a little slumming expedition. I'll promise to take good care of you."

He leaned toward her, tremulous, expectant. Honey's beauty was of a sort to stir men deeply. More than beauty, perhaps—a vital charm that appealed to primitive instincts; the more compelling because she was unconscious of it. Thus it happened that, when she flashed a glance into Mr. Ogden's eyes, he suddenly felt a keen desire to shield her, to protect her from contact with the world. But for the presence of his chauffeur, he would have taken her in his arms. As it was, he compromised by placing his hand gently upon her knee.

"Do you think I ought to go—with you?" Honey said uneasily. "Your wife—"

"A man has some privileges nowadays," Mr. Ogden replied, "even if he is married. Mrs. Ogden, I am sure, would not enjoy a cabaret. You would. If you have nothing else to do tomorrow night—"

LOVE'S GREATEST MISTAKE 137

"I—I don't know," Honey told him, suddenly afraid. "I'll think it over."

When she reached home, she called up Mona Terry and asked her advice. Of late she had come to depend on the latter a great deal.

"Certainly I'd go," Miss Terry told her. "Why not please him? There's no harm in it. Make him your friend. The world isn't so conventional as it used to be. And look here, Honey. When he suggests supper, say you'd like to go to the Red Peacock. Say you've heard about it from friends. Ray and I will be on hand, to look after you. I'm a girl from your home town, understand, working in the movies. That sounds better than the shop. And Ray's the man I'm going to marry—a well known scenario writer. Get me? Tell him we're going to be there—see—otherwise he might think it queer, your meeting people by accident in a place to which you've never been. If this man takes an interest in you—a fatherly interest, understand—your future's assured."

Honey thought over Mona's advice for a long time before she went to sleep. She certainly did not wish to offend Mr. Ogden by seeming puritanical, narrow. If only he hadn't touched her knee!

138 LOVE'S GREATEST MISTAKE

Mr. Ogden sent for her the next afternoon, at about half-past four, ostensibly to point out some corrections in a contract she had typed. When she was alone with him, he made no reference to it.

"You're going, of course," he said, standing very close to her.

Honey saw that his hands trembled, that there were lines beneath his eyes.

"Why—yes—I think so," she nodded.

Then, quite suddenly, before she realized his intention, he took her in his arms, pressed swift and violent kisses upon her hair, her lips.

"Fatherly interest," Mona Terry had said. There was nothing fatherly about Mr. Ogden now. She struggled from his arms.

When a man has kissed a woman against her will, there is only one excuse he may offer without offending her—that he could not help it, that her irresistible sweetness and charm made him lose his head.

This excuse Mr. Ogden, after his sudden embrace, offered Honey, and because it happened to be true she believed him—forgave him. If he had tried to kiss her again, she would have fled from his office. As it was, she did her best to relieve an awkward situation.

LOVE'S GREATEST MISTAKE 139

"You said we might be—friends," she told him. "I'd be glad of that. But—anything else—"

"I know. I understand. If I were twenty years younger—"

"It isn't that—really it isn't," Honey interrupted. "I like you ever so much just as you are. You don't seem—old to me. And I'm not a hypocrite. I've been kissed before—often. Only—with you, it's different. You're married, for one thing. And you have lots of money, and that makes you think that you can buy anything you want; even—people. I hoped, if I went out with you tonight, that you could forget those things—and—"

"I can. We'll pretend I'm not married at all; that I'm just a hard-working young clerk on a small salary; and we'll use taxicabs instead of my car."

He was all eagerness, now that Honey once more smiled.

"I've engaged a table at a delightful little restaurant, and tickets for a musical show you'll like. As for supper, there are a number of interesting places: the Valencia, for instance, or the Red Peacock. I've been there once or twice."

"Wherever you say," Honey told him, marveling that he had mentioned the very place Mona had suggested. There was nothing marvelous about it, however, since the Red Peacock was the most popular night club of the hour.

"Very well. And you won't mind meeting me at the restaurant, will you, in time for dinner? About seven, let us say." He wrote for a moment on a slip of paper. "Here's the address. You'd better take a taxi there."

Honey went back to her desk, a little frightened, a little thrilled. To be taken to dinner, the theater, supper, by so wealthy and important a man!

With a sinking heart she realized that she had nothing to wear worthy of so great an occasion. Once more she would be obliged to apply to Jane. Would she never have any pretty things of her own?

Far back in her brain a small voice whispered that, under certain conditions, Mr. Ogden would be very glad to buy her all the pretty things she wanted.

He complimented her enthusiastically when she met him at the restaurant, and continued

LOVE'S GREATEST MISTAKE

his flattering remarks throughout dinner and the play.

Honey, in daringly cut white satin trimmed with lace, was breath-taking—a provocative saint; a white passion flower; a Sleeping Beauty awaiting the passionate embraces of the Prince. It pleased Mr. Ogden to fancy himself that prince.

He was not alone in his admiration. At the Red Peacock, a score of jaded, world-weary eyes were fixed gloatingly on Honey's young beauty. Mr. Ogden sat down, very proud because he knew he was being envied.

Honey glanced around the place, disappointed. She had expected something vaguely, impossibly different. She saw only a room hung in jade-green velvet, decorated everywhere with fantastic red peacocks. Even the china and glassware bore these birds.

Instead of a joyous, bacchanalian crowd, she found herself surrounded by hard-eyed, wolfish men or silly, stupid ones; by calculating women; by smart, jaded boys, many of them tipsy, but all affecting a noisy gayety that even Honey, inexperienced though she was, could see came from nervous stimulation, not from the heart—a sort of crazy, jumping-jack gayety unpleasant to witness. A dreadful merry-go-round whirling endlessly to a mad, pagan tune.

From hostess to bus boy, the whole machinery of the place was organized for one purpose—to extract from its patrons the last dollar they had to spend.

Mr. Ogden danced with Honey once, smoothly, in an old-fashioned way quite unlike the gyrations of the couples around them. The passion that lay in the music caused him, however, to hold her closely—so closely, indeed, that Honey could feel the hard pressure of the buttons of his coat against her breast; could even sense the more rapid beating of his heart.

The contact left her cold. If she had been in Don's arms—Yet she liked Mr. Ogden better now than she had at any time since their first meeting. He treated her as he might have treated a woman of his own class. A subtle form of flattery.

They had barely returned to their table when Mona and Ray Becker appeared. Certain changes in their dress, their manner, caused Honey to lift her eyebrows. Mona, her mop of red hair restrained by a bandeau, wore almost no make-up. Her modest evening gown was of black taffeta. Gone were her French jewelry, her slang. She seemed as demure as Honey herself.

Mr. Becker, quiet, reserved, portrayed admirably the part of a serious-minded writer. The patent-leather polish had disappeared from his hair. He had even donned eyeglasses with a wide silk ribbon.

When Honey introduced them, Mr. Ogden suggested that they sit down. There was some trivial conversation between Mona and Honey about their home town, while Ray expounded to Mr. Ogden his theory that what the motion-picture industry needed most was the co-operation of able authors—men of ideas, like himself.

Presently he asked Honey to dance.

When they had whirled off, Mona became pensive.

"A wonderful girl, Honey," she confided to Mr. Ogden. "Sweet and fresh as a flower. I often wonder what she is going to make of herself here in New York, with its temptations, its mad life. She tells me you have been very kind to her, Mr. Ogden."

"Not at all. I've given her a small position in my office, and she has filled it well. Earned all we've paid her—and more. A charming girl. And a good one."

"Yes. Honey's straight as a string. She admires you very much, Mr. Ogden."

"How do you know that?" He was flattered, but cautious.

"She's told me. Over and over. To her, you are everything that is worth while—an ideal man."

"Really." Mr. Ogden tried to seem incredulous, but his vanity was tickled. "You think she honestly likes me, then—for myself?"

"Of course. Why shouldn't she? I don't know anything about you, Mr. Ogden, except what Honey has told me. My interests are all in the screen. My work, you know. But I love Honey. We have been friends ever since we were children. I know how she looks up to you—admires you. She's never tired of talking about it. Be good to her, Mr. Ogden. I ask it, as an old friend. You know the world. Help her to go straight, to make something of herself. She can, with the right opportunities. Ray—Mr. Becker—thinks she has a wonderful future in pictures."

This appeal, delivered with consummate skill, left Mr. Ogden under the not disagreeable impression that Honey was infatuated with him and that her future lay in his hands. It made him feel like a god—a middle-aged god.

When Honey and Ray returned to the table, Mona excused herself and took Honey with her to the dressing-room.

"He's perfectly adorable," she gushed. "And mad about you. He told me so. Thinks you're wonderful. You certainly have made a hit with him. I wish I had a friend like that."

"Friend!" Honey laughed. "This afternoon, at the office, he tried to kiss me."

"Well, why not? Any man would who wasn't dead on his feet. Let him have a kiss once in a while. It will make him feel young again. Not very often, of course. And don't kiss him back. That would be fatal. In a week or two you'll have him eating out of your hand."

"But—I don't want him eating out of my hand. What for? There's nothing Mr. Ogden can do for me—nothing I want him to do—except raise my salary."

Mona lifted her eyebrows in an incredulous stare.

"Nothing he can do for you? How do you

get that way? With his money, he can do everything for you. Back you in pictures! Make you a celebrity! Build you a theater! Anything! For heaven's sake, don't be such a dumb-bell. Play your cards right. Keep him guessing. Work the innocent-little-girl stuff for all it's worth.''

Honey faced her, clear-eyed.

"I don't have to work anything, Mona. I'm straight. You know that."

"So much the better. You've got something he wants. Make him want it enough and he'll give anything in the world to get it."

The anger in Honey's eyes increased.

"Look here, Mona," she said. "I'm no gold-digger."

"Shucks! All women are, in one way or another. Some girls fall for a round of drinks. A rope of pearls might land me—if it weren't for Ray. If your price is marriage, so much the better. No trouble to get rid of a wife nowadays. Whatever you're after, the principle's the same. Shall we go back?"

At the table, Ray Becker, with many expressions of a technical nature, was explaining to Mr. Ogden that Honey, with the proper "vehicle," might readily become a highly successful screen star. He planned to write a picture for her.

When she returned, Mr. Ogden eyed her with new respect.

Food, absurdly costly, none too well prepared, littered the table. Champagne, at staggering prices, was poured out, wasted. Neither Mr. Ogden nor Honey drank much of it; but Ray and Mona, their work now done, displayed astonishing appetites. At an interval in the cabaret performance, Mr. Ogden glanced at his watch.

"Three o'clock," he said. "Time for all little girls to be in bed."

Both Mona and Ray, to Honey's surprise, seconded the suggestion.

"Better get your beauty sleep, dear," the former said. "Give me a ring in the morning."

Honey found the fresh night air grateful after the hot atmosphere of the café. A cab whirled Mr. Ogden and her swiftly to Jane's door. In the vestibule, he gripped her hand, but made no attempt to embrace her.

"It's been—wonderful—having you," he whispered. "Good night—you dear."

Then, without realizing it, Honey played a master stroke.

"You've been awfully sweet to me," she said, and kissed him swiftly, softly on the lips—the kiss of a child.

An instant later she had disappeared through the doorway.

Mr. Ogden returned to his cab feeling twenty years younger. As he drove downtown he hummed a very gay tune.

CHAPTER XVI

ONE afternoon a week or so later, Honey met Herbert Gibbs as she was leaving the office. It was the first time she had seen him since their quarrel. He had telephoned that he would call for her.

"My mother and sisters are in town," he said. "Been to a wedding. I told them I'd bring you up for tea."

He helped Honey into a cab.

On the way uptown he did not refer in any way to their disagreement over Mr. Ogden. He seemed in a joyous mood, which Honey liked.

"Adorable," he whispered. "New York is agreeing with you. You're lovelier than ever, and I'm crazier about you. What have you been doing with yourself this past week?"

Honey could not face him with her usual frankness. Since the evening at the Red Peacock she had lunched with Mr. Ogden twice, gone to a matinée, and for a long and quite wonderful drive out on Long Island for dinner. Remembering that her anger with Herbert had been caused by his suggestion that Mr. Ogden might try to make love to her, she met his smiling gaze a bit unsteadily.

"I haven't been doing anything in particular," she replied. And when Herbert tried to take her hand she drew it away in sudden annoyance—not with him, but with herself. Then she put it back again. After all, she had done nothing wrong. And Herbert *was* nice. Homely, and awkward, and shy, but—nice. She thought of their momentary kiss in the cab a week before, and smiled. He had not been shy then. But she did not permit him to kiss her again, although he attempted it.

"Silly—not in broad daylight!" she laughed; then repaid him with one of her glowing smiles.

Honey liked Lovey Gibbs, Herbert's young and tomboyish sister, when she met her in the lounge of the hotel on Forty-second Street. Mrs. Gibbs, tall, elegant, aristocratic, gave the girl a swift, shrewd look, and found herself baffled.

Herbert had talked about Honey enough to arouse his mother's fears. She had supposed her boy the last person in the world to become interested in a stenographer—seriously inter-

LOVE'S GREATEST MISTAKE 151

ested, that is. The Gibbs men simply did not do such things. They had too much ancestral pride. But there were no telltale shadows in Honey's eyes—she met the older woman's questioning gaze fearlessly.

Josephine, Herbert's older sister, was a replica of her mother—the same attitude of being just a trifle above the ordinary run of mankind. But Lovey was disgracefully, adorably human, and frankly admired Honey for the simple reason that she was earning her own living.

"I'm fed up on all this bunk about what my great-great-grandfather did," she confided. "I want to get out and do something myself."

"Mother and the girls want me to bring you out to the place sometime soon," Herbert said.

"I'd love to come," Honey told him, and glanced at Mrs. Gibbs.

"Why not Sunday?" the latter suggested. "If it's a nice day."

"Sunday it is. Early." Herbert was beaming. "Honey—Miss McNeill—is anxious for a swim."

"I can do a hundred yards with my hands tied behind my back," Lovey announced proudly.

152 LOVE'S GREATEST MISTAKE

Mrs. Gibbs glanced at her watch.

"I'm afraid we'll have to go," she said. "Our train leaves in fifteen minutes. Tell the waiter to bring the check."

"Isn't she a dear?" Herbert whispered.

"Quite lovely," the old lady whispered back. "Exteriorly, at least. What's inside I haven't an idea. Have you?"

"I should say I have. Look at her eyes."

"Eyes, my boy, tell nothing. The worst woman I ever knew could look at you like an angel from heaven and lie like a trooper while doing it."

"Your mother didn't like me," Honey said, when they had gone. "I wonder why."

"That's easy. She thinks I'm falling in love with you."

"Nonsense. We're just—friends."

Herbert grasped her hand as they walked through the station. His fingers were trembling.

"Oh—hell!" he said. "If only we were—somewhere else. Let's go over to my apartment and—talk. There's something I want to say to you."

Honey shook her head.

"Your mother would dislike me more than

ever," she laughed, "if I did a thing like that. Besides, I told my sister I'd be home for dinner."

Mr. Ogden watched Honey hungrily across the little rose-lit table. It had alternately annoyed and rejoiced him that he could feel like a schoolboy in the presence of this girl less than half his age—could lie awake at night for hours thinking of her—could rise in the morning with her name on his lips—could dream of moonlit rose gardens, of tropic beaches, of all the romantic things he had not dreamed of for years. Was it just a mad infatuation? Or was he honestly in love? He found it difficult to decide.

"I'm going away tomorrow, Honey dear," he said presently. "Will you miss me?"

"How could I help it," Honey smiled, "after all your kindness? Are you going to be away long?"

"Three weeks at least. Mrs. Ogden isn't so well. The doctor wants her to spend the autumn on the Riviera. I shall cross with her, spend a few days attending to some business in Paris, and return by the next boat."

"I wish I were going!" Honey said, without thinking. A trip to Europe was one of her pet dreams, as it had been one of her father's.

"I wish to God you were!" Mr. Ogden exclaimed. He too had been dreaming. "You shall, some day—with me."

He seized her hand as it lay upon the table.

"You know I care for you, dear. I can't think of anybody else. And you won't let me do a thing for you. With all my money, I'm helpless. I'd ask you to marry me if I were free, but I'm not. I can't be—ever—not while my wife lives. You see, I respect her. She's a fine woman. But I can't feel toward her the way I do toward you.

"Honey, the world's a hopeless place. We all dream and struggle for happiness, and when it comes we—throw it away. Conventions are what hold us back, of course—like millstones around our necks. I don't want to suggest anything wrong—anything the world would call wrong—but why shouldn't we be happy together? I'm a very rich man. I used to think I could buy happiness. I know now I can't. But you can give it to me—if you will. And in return I'll give you—love and everything else in the world you could possibly want. Everything! Without limit. Do you like me well enough for that?"

LOVE'S GREATEST MISTAKE 155

He was not explicit, but Honey understood. A certain sincerity in his manner made it impossible for her to take offense. She faced the situation frankly. She was to become his mistress—in return for unlimited wealth. Unlimited, because she knew that in his present mood Mr. Ogden would care nothing for the price he paid to secure the happiness he so greatly desired. His next words assured her of that.

"I'll give you an income of your own," he whispered, "a large income—whatever sum you wish—for the rest of your life. To be yours, no matter what happens. I love you, Honey, desperately—with all my heart."

Mona Terry's cynical advice flashed through Honey's mind: "Don't let them fool you with promises—get certified checks." And Jane's bitter comments on married poverty—her questionable methods of escape from it: flirting with Don, with romance, as an antidote to domestic boredom. It almost stunned her to realize that, with a word, she could make herself rich—very rich.

Money was power. New York had shown her that. Between thirty dollars a week and $30,000 a year stood merely an idea. Many women had brushed it aside and received the plaudits of the crowd.

She had no one to consider but herself. And Mr. Ogden loved her—for the time being, at least.

Women married for money. Why was it any less honorable to accept money without marriage? A bargain, either way!

Association with a man by no means disagreeable to her—a man of breadth, of unusual charm, a man of whom she was rather fond. Not as she had been fond of Don Kendall. But Don's pagan arms, she feared, would have crushed her, left her helpless.

As for Herbert Gibbs, with his meager income, his dreams of winning fame and fortune at a stroke—she might marry him and his poverty, but would she not in the end be like Jane? With a "nice little home" somewhere in the suburbs, and—boredom?

Mr. Ogden's offer meant life—life in its broadest, fullest sense: luxury; travel. Never a moment of worry as long as she lived. The world at her feet.

Of course, she had wanted youth—the mating of youth, but—

she said, "where a rich oil man in St. Louis took a girl out of a candy shop and made an opera singer of her. Sent her abroad to study, and everything. He had a wife, too. If you promised to write, Honey, I think you ought to do it."

Whereupon Honey, bored with lying in bed, composed a harmless little note that anyone might have read. Mona did read it—and promptly tore it up.

"Put some pep into your letter, for heaven's sake!" she exclaimed. "And tell him about your illness. Play it up strong. Say you're threatened with pneumonia. Girls get diamonds for less than that."

Honey rewrote the letter; but the most she would admit was that she had a bad cold. It was Mona who, taking the letter to post, steamed it open and added a lurid postscript to the effect that Honey was dangerously ill, but that Mrs. Sommers and she were doing their best to take care of her.

Mr. Ogden, reading the letter in his Paris hotel, felt his middle-aged heart skip several beats.

He was desperately fond of Honey. Her youth and her beauty held him, even with the breadth of the Atlantic between them. That very morning he had told a friend that he hadn't seen a good-looking woman since he had arrived in Europe.

It was perhaps to be expected that during his remaining five days in Paris, lonely, worried, eager to return, he should have sent Honey two cablegrams and written her three ardent letters.

Ostrichlike, he signed all three letters with his initials only. As if he could hope to deny his bold and characteristic handwriting!

In his cablegrams he expressed extreme anxiety over Honey's illness, advised calling in a specialist, directed her to apply to Mr. Roder for money.

In his letters he told her of his love, of his unhappiness without her, of his eagerness to return and be with her once more.

Foolish, perhaps. Yet Mr. Ogden was no fool. He knew that Honey was a woman to be trusted. He could not know that Mona had surreptitiously read the letters and promptly reported their contents to Ray Becker.

"I want those letters, and I want 'em quick!" Ray snarled at her. "We've got the old bird where he can't move a finger except to

LOVE'S GREATEST MISTAKE 161

write a nice fat check. Hop to it, angel-face—and make it snappy!"

"How do you expect me to get them?" Mona rebelled. "They're hid. And she'd never give them up, if I asked her."

Mr. Becker sat in deep silence for several minutes. When he spoke, it was with decision.

"First you go to her—see—and tell her there's a wad of jack in this thing for all of us. She needn't appear in any way. All she's got to do is to say the letters were lost—stolen. That lets her out. We'll split three ways. She ought to cop out a hundred thousand for her share. Fix her for life, and nobody the wiser.

"You know damned well she isn't going to fall for Ogden's offer to keep her. When she tells him so, he'll give her the air. Why shouldn't she come out of the thing with a fat bank roll and still keep her virtue, if that's what's worrying her? I believe she'll do it."

"I don't," said Mona, "but I'll try it."

Which she did, very cleverly, very subtly, with no mention of anything so crude as blackmail.

Honey heard her through.

"Of course I won't give you the letters, Mona Terry!" she exclaimed angrily. "You and Ray have been planning this thing from the start. I was a fool not to see it. Mr. Ogden has trusted me. I'd be a fine piece of work, wouldn't I, to throw him down! Let you two blackmail him!"

"Oh, don't be so dramatic! The old fool's had dozens of women before you. Why shouldn't he cough up a few hundred thousand? He'd never miss it. And he deserves anything he gets."

Honey refused to be placated.

"If that's what your friendship means, Mona," she exclaimed, "I'm through with you! I'm going to keep the letters until Mr. Ogden comes back from Europe, and then give them to him myself."

Their talk had taken place in Mona's apartment. Honey, recovered from her illness, had stopped there in response to a telephone call on her way uptown.

She left in a gust of anger.

When Ray Becker appeared from the adjoining bedroom, Mona faced him with a sullen stare.

"I told you it wouldn't work," she said.

Mr. Becker eyed her with supreme contempt.

"You're about as much use to me," he

growled, "as a safety razor to a bearded lady. From now on I'm going to handle this thing myself!"

The more Honey reflected upon the muck through which her association with Mona Terry had dragged her, the angrier she became. Partnership in a blackmailing scheme! The thought of it left her raging. How could Mona—how could anyone—suppose she would be willing to take advantage of the trust Mr. Ogden had placed in her?

She began to understand, now, why Mona and Ray Becker had been so eager to have her "play up" to him—could follow all their devious moves, from her first visit to Mr. Ogden's office down to Mona's insistence that she should write to him about her illness while he was abroad. A slimy, degrading business! She longed for someone to restore her self-respect, and turned to Herbert Gibbs. Slow he might be, but at least he stood for the decent, honorable things of life.

As for Mr. Ogden, she could scarcely wait for him to return—he was expected daily—in order that she might have opportunity to hand him back his letters. As for the left-handed love he had offered her, she wanted none of it, nor the money that went with it. In her present austere frame of mind, the whole affair sickened her.

Of Don Kendall she thought much, and always with the same longing to see him—to be near him. Whether he had returned to town or not, she did not know, and she made no attempt to find out. If Mr. Ogden's offer to buy her love had been degrading, so might Don's passionate and pagan love-making be. She felt afraid of him—of herself. Herbert Gibbs she could trust, even though he failed to thrill her.

The visit to Stamford that she had promised to make had been put off because of her illness. Herbert had sent her flowers and telephoned frequently to ask about her. His little attentions pleased Honey greatly. She began to wonder whether life might not be largely made up of such simple, homely things, rather than of tremendous thrills.

The day for the drive to Stamford was finally set, and Herbert called for her in his roadster. For some reason, Honey had pictured the Gibbs homestead as a very modest place. The reality surprised her. A graveled drive, shaded by old and very beautiful elms and oaks, wound through thick shrubbery to

A Paramount Picture. HONEY AND HARVEY KISS AND MAKE UP—TEMPORARILY. *Love's Greatest Mistake.*

LOVE'S GREATEST MISTAKE

the house, a long low affair of clapboards and shingles. The porch, with its screen of honeysuckle and wistaria, was delightful.

The spacious rooms within were filled with old-fashioned furniture, their floors of wide, dark planks covered with deep-pile rugs. With the book-lined study overlooking a terraced garden at the rear, Honey felt particularly delighted. The stone fireplace in the living-room, Josephine explained to her, had been built more than a hundred years before. Lovey, Herbert's young sister, made fun of it all, much to Josephine's annoyance.

"What's the use of having ancestors, if you don't live up to them?" Lovey said, sticking out her tongue at one family portrait. "Great-grandpa Philip was a good old egg. Arrested once for smuggling, I'm told. And Great-aunt Eliza Martin ran off with a sea captain and had a perfectly gorgeous time in China."

Josephine's attempts to silence her were futile.

"Some day," she announced, "I shall beat it for Cairo and find myself a nice, good-looking sheik. Want to go along, Miss McNeill?"

"Call me Honey, won't you?" the latter said. "Everybody does."

"Yes—I've noticed it."

The youngster grinned at Herbert as he appeared in a ragged sweater and a disgraceful pair of plus fours.

"Come along," he announced. "It's a six-mile drive to the beach. Back for dinner at two. Your suit's in the car, Honey."

The three of them clattered out. Mrs. Gibbs and Josephine gazed solemnly at each other.

"Very pretty," the former observed. "Good, I think. But there is something I don't understand about her."

"No use arguing with Herbert," Josephine replied. "He's as stubborn as ten mules. I think he means to marry her."

This latter remark, as it happened, was true. Herbert had decided upon that. The swim over, he led Honey to the shelter of a lifeboat drawn up on the beach. There they lingered in the sunshine for a time.

CHAPTER XVIII

AFTER dinner he undertook to show Honey the rose garden. He guided her, finally, to a stone bench, drew her to a seat beside him.

"Look here, you adorable creature," he said, with his dry smile, "don't you know you ought to get married?"

"Why?" Honey asked, a bit startled.

"Because no one as devastatingly beautiful as you are has any right to be running around loose, tempting impressionable bachelors to lose their heads."

"Do you really think I'm dangerous?"

"Dangerous! You're a positive menace to the peace of mind of the community—especially to mine. Something's got to be done about it."

"What would you suggest?"

"That you marry me, of course. It's the only thing you can do, as I see it."

He spoke so whimsically that Honey scarcely knew whether to take him seriously or not.

"This is so sudden!" she mocked. "Give me time, Herbert dear, to think it over."

168 LOVE'S GREATEST MISTAKE

"All right. I want you to think it over. I make a hundred a week. That's all. Marrying a man with an income as small as that deserves to be thought over—seriously. It means sacrifices—lots of them. I oughtn't to ask them of you. Wouldn't—if I did not love you so much. Do you know that? I didn't, until recently. Not quite. I suspected it, though. Of course, any girl with your looks should marry millions. Fool if she doesn't. You'd be throwing yourself away on me. But I love you, Honey darling. When you think things over, remember that."

Honey waited for Herbert to sweep her into his arms. Men usually did, when they proposed. Her companion, however, made no such attempt—merely continued to regard her with his singularly grave smile.

"I'm not going to urge you into this thing —to try to take you by storm," he said slowly; "by kissing you—all that. I want you to decide matters for yourself. If you find that you care for me enough to marry me—to share my —poverty—it's almost that you know, in New York, these days—why, tell me so. I don't believe you'd regret it. But I think a woman should decide such things sensibly, and not under the influence of passion—with somebody's lips against hers. Too many marriages are made that way. Moonlight—romance—kisses. Marriage isn't all romance. You've got to think of the morning after. I'm going to give you one week to make up your mind."

Honey heard him in silence. There seemed, in fact, nothing she could say. No doubt his ideas about marriage were correct enough, but they left her chilled. She could not help comparing the businesslike methods of Herbert Gibbs with the whirlwind love-making of Don Kendall—Don, who was all passion, all romance, leaving consequences to take care of themselves.

A little puzzled, a little bewildered, she looked up to see Lovey coming down the path toward them.

"Sorry to interrupt, but tea's ready!" She was grinning impishly.

"We'd better go along," Herbert said. "Mother is a bit particular about being on time at meals."

There was something in the way he spoke that made Honey feel very sure the Gibbs family lived, ordered all the events of their lives, from births to deaths, in a precise and punctual way. Practical—but hardly exciting.

On the drive back to town, Herbert made no further reference to his proposal, but chatted on about his work, his love for the country, for the old place they had just left. It was close on 10 o'clock when they drew up at Jane's door. Herbert shook her hand as he might have shaken that of a dear friend.

"Good night, Honey," he whispered. "I hope your answer is going to be yes."

Honey climbed the stairs to her sister's apartment, feeling that the day had somehow been a failure. It was very fine, very noble on Herbert's part, no doubt, to be unwilling to sway her through her emotions; but—there was such a thing as being *too* cold-blooded.

Engrossed in her thoughts, she pushed open the apartment door. Then, as the lock clicked behind her, something occurred that left her limp, gasping.

A man came between the curtains of the living-room door—a man wearing a black mask. In his hand was an automatic pistol, its blue muzzle close to Honey's breast.

She tried to scream, but her attempt was smothered by lean, talon-like fingers closing swiftly about her throat.

CHAPTER XIX

THE puppets that made up Honey's small world had danced fantastically, that Sunday night, to create the situation by which she was faced on her return from the Gibbs place at Stamford.

There was Jane, for example. Jane had said she was not going out. But the hot, lonely afternoon left her restless, bored; and when Mona Terry called up a little after four and suggested a drive to Long Beach, Jane was delighted. They could have a swim, Mona said, and dance afterward. Some friends were taking her down. She did not mention Ray Becker as one of the party, although he was standing beside the telephone when she spoke.

"You simply *must* come," Mona insisted. "We'll stop by for you in half an hour. That will give you time to get dressed."

Jane, however, was already dressed—dressed and waiting in the vain hope that Don Kendall might happen to call. He had frequently done so on Sunday afternoons in the past. She knew he had been out of town, of course—but he should be back by now.

When she left, she stuck a card in the little box in the vestibule, with a few words penciled on it to the effect that she would be back about 10 o'clock.

Jane having been thus disposed of, the powers that be turned their attention to the case of Don Kendall.

That restless young man, grown suddenly sick of the night life of New York, had gone to Canada on a fishing trip—roughing it, with some men friends, in the open. He wanted to think where the air was serene, away from the eternal throb of jazz. Just what he wanted to think about was not clear, even to himself; but he found, when he got there, that it was Honey.

Her vivid young beauty confronted him constantly, mirrored in still lakes, wreathed in fantastic clouds. It annoyed him, in a way, that he could not get the girl out of his mind. But, finding escape impossible, he suddenly packed up his fishing gear, bade his friends a curt good-by, and left for New York as quickly as he could.

It was Sunday night when he arrived—early in the evening.

LOVE'S GREATEST MISTAKE 173

Being a man of action, he jumped into a cab and drove at once to Jane's apartment. The card, with its penciled message that Mrs. Sommers would be back about 10 o'clock confronted him as he was about to ring the bell. Assuming that Honey was with her sister, he hurried home, bathed and changed, and went to his club for a late dinner.

He wanted to see Honey very much indeed. Otherwise he would have waited until the morning. He wanted to see her, to find out whether the vision of the mirrored lakes was, after all, only a vision or a flesh-and-blood reality. He knew, from past experience, that absence frequently tends towards exaggeration —that the Honey of his dreams might prove to be, when he met her face to face, merely an attractive but unimportant young girl.

He almost hoped it would turn out that way. Don Kendall loved freedom. It irked him to realize that any woman could completely dominate his thoughts. With a vast deal of impatience, he waited for 10 o'clock to arrive.

Meanwhile, Honey, in her sister's apartment, faced a crisis of which she had little dreamed. The appearance of the masked man, and her utter helplessness in his grasp, left her all but paralyzed with fright.

Her first thought was of burglars—her call for help a natural reaction to that thought. But when her cries were stopped by the man's fingers, closing like claws around her throat, she could only struggle blindly, hopelessly, against his superior strength.

One bewildered glance, as she was being dragged into the living-room, confirmed her first impression—that the place had been entered by thieves. She was aware of books and papers scattered over the floor—of confusion, disorder. Then she was flung on a couch. Collecting her whirling senses, she looked up, to find the man in the mask standing over her, speaking in a voice that seemed to her strangely familiar.

"Where are those letters from Ogden?" he snarled.

"Ray!" Honey's exclamation was almost a scream—yet she could not be sure because of the mask.

The man paid no attention to her cries.

"Where are they? I want them—quick!"

Honey struggled to a sitting position, frightened, weak.

LOVE'S GREATEST MISTAKE

"I haven't—I can't let you—"

"Don't try to kid me. Just hand over those letters, or"—once more her assailant's slim fingers reached talon-like for her throat.

"No," she shook her head wearily. "I can't."

Her purse lay beside the couch. The man, catching sight of it, snatched it up and tore it open, so that its small and unimportant contents were scattered upon the floor. Then, with a cry of rage, he seized Honey by the wrist and, whirling her to her feet, began to strip off the sport suit she wore.

In a moment the girl stood in her undergarments, a pitiful, trembling figure. The attack upon her had revealed no hidden letters. But Honey was now filled with other and more poignant fears. She darted toward the bedroom. If she could reach it she might lock herself in!

Her assailant, however, was too quick. Seizing her arm, he bent it behind her, twisting it in a cruel hammer lock. Rage gleamed in his narrowed eyes. Anger and disappointment rasped in his voice.

"Tell me where they are," he snapped, "or I'll twist your damned arm off!"

"No!" Honey said dully.

A wave of pain like a crimson flood rose in her brain. The letters Mr. Ogden had written her were so close to where she stood that she might have reached out and touched them. But —he had trusted her.

"No!" she gasped, struggling against the pain.

"The hell you won't!" the man growled, giving her arm another twist. "Come on, damn you! Out with it!"

Honey was biting and scratching, now, in her agony.

"No!" she whispered. "I won't do it. I won't."

The waves of pain rose higher, threatening to engulf her senses; but still she managed to resist—to shake her head.

Then the man gave her wrist another deadly turn, and Honey fainted. It was as if the crimson flood in her brain had burst its bounds and drowned her. As she pitched to the floor, she was mercifully unaware that her assailant, in a flare of anger, savagely kicked her.

Fate, having finished for the moment with Honey, now turned its attention to Don Kendall. That young man was driving swiftly across Eighty-second Street, on his way to Jane's apartment. A glance at the lighted windows told him that someone was in.

As he stepped into the vestibule, looking for Mrs. Sommers' bell, a woman passed him, opening the front door with a latchkey. Don followed her up the stairs. At the landing of Honey's floor he glanced down the corridor. A man was just leaving the apartment—a slender, black-haired man, handsome in a vulgar, sleek way. He seemed hurried, angry, as he slammed the door after him and went down the stairs. Some friend of Honey's sister, no doubt, Don thought, as he pressed the bell at the apartment door. The man's face was vaguely familiar.

At first there was no answer to the bell, no sound from within. Don waited for a moment, a grim expression on his clean-cut face.

"Honey!" he cried, leaning his six-foot-two of muscle against the panels of the door. "Is anything wrong?"

He was prepared to burst his way in.

From the silence presently emerged sounds —footsteps—the smooth click of a lock. Then the door moved inward swiftly under the pressure of Don's shoulder. He gazed around him, gasping. Honey stood in the tiny hallway, a

178 LOVE'S GREATEST MISTAKE

disheveled and pathetic figure, her clothing torn to shreds.

Dazed by fright and pain, she had struggled to her feet on hearing the pounding at the door. The thought that help had come gave her quick strength.

Don's amazement gave way to rage. It was confounding enough to find Honey standing thus unclothed before him, but what of the sleek young man he had passed in the corridor —the man who had but a moment before left the apartment? Staring surprised and angry into Honey's flushed face, Don could not know that her left arm had been almost wrenched from its socket—that she was suffering intense and bewildering pain.

"Who was the man that just left here?" he demanded. "And where is your sister?"

"She's—out," Honey whispered.

Then she saw the rage in Don's eyes—the amazement as they fell for a moment to her bare breasts. In quick shame she moved her arms to cover herself, forgetting her injured shoulder.

The sudden spasm of pain that shot through her seared like a hot iron. With a choking sob, she fell into Don's arms.

LOVE'S GREATEST MISTAKE

The contact with her soft, warm body, the tender weight of her, the perfume of her flesh, left Don Kendall almost as dazed as she was herself. He knew nothing of her injuries, but her expression told him a story of devastating pain and fear. Lifting her clear of the floor, he carried her into the living-room and laid her upon the couch. For a brief moment he stood, gazing down at her tender and exquisite beauty. Then, in sudden shame, he went into the bedroom, and, returning with a counterpane, flung it over her.

There was a pitcher of water on the table. He dashed its contents into Honey's face and began to rub her hands, her arms frantically. When she opened her eyes, he questioned her.

"What is wrong, dear?" he asked. "Has someone hurt you?"

"It was—I think it was—" Honey whispered. Then terror sealed her lips.

She could not explain her assailant's presence without admitting the truth about Mr. Ogden's letters. And, even in her agony, she did not want Don to know about them. He would never understand.

"There was a man here," she murmured, "when I came in." She could scarcely speak,

180 LOVE'S GREATEST MISTAKE

being sick with pain. "He had a pistol. When I screamed, fought, he tore my clothes off—wrenched my arm. A burglar, I think."

For the first time Don Kendall saw the scattered books and papers on the floor.

"You poor kid!" he muttered, kneeling beside the couch. But when he sought to take her in his arms, to press quick kisses against her lips, Honey cried out in sudden agony.

Don sprang to his feet.

"For God's sake, tell me what has happened!" he exclaimed.

"It—it's my arm," Honey moaned. "He twisted it. I—I fainted. And something hurts me terribly—here." She pressed her side, her lips gray with pain.

"Good God!" Don exclaimed. "Why didn't you let me know? I'll get a doctor at once!"

Then Jane arrived, bursting in suddenly to find Honey stretched upon the couch, with Don standing beside her. A glance at her sister's gray and agonized face put new fears into Jane's heart.

"Honey! What's wrong?" she asked quickly.

"Someone broke in," Don replied, "and attacked her. I found her like this."

LOVE'S GREATEST MISTAKE

"Oh!" Jane rushed to her sister's side. "Who was it? Tell me."

"I don't think I'd bother about who it was just now, Mrs. Sommers," Don said curtly. "What your sister needs is a doctor."

"There's one in the apartment at the corner. I've been to him. Named Miller."

Jane sprang to the telephone. The doctor was luckily in and would come over at once.

When he did, and had made a quick examination, he gave Honey a tablet to ease her pain, then took Don and Jane into the next room.

"Her shoulder is badly wrenched—ligaments torn—will have to be put in a cast," he said. "Nothing dangerous about that. As for the pain in her side, I can't tell. Ribs fractured, with possible internal injuries. Needs an X-ray examination to be sure. My advice is to send her to a hospital at once."

Don and Jane stared gravely at each other.

"Can you arrange it?" the latter asked.

"Don't know about a room. She may have to go into the emergency ward," replied the doctor. "May I use your telephone?"

An hour later an ambulance deposited Honey at Roosevelt Hospital.

CHAPTER XX

Mr. William Ogden, returning from Europe that morning, went at once to his office. He arrived, as usual, by way of his private entrance, and seated himself at his desk. He summoned his secretary and asked to see Mr. Roder.

The latter came in, a newspaper in his hand. "Ah—how do you do, Roder?" Mr. Ogden asked, as casually as he could with pictures of Honey's face drifting before his eyes. The three weeks abroad had not chilled his passion. He could scarcely wait to see her.

"I trust you had a pleasant trip, sir," Mr. Roder remarked, placing some documents upon his employer's desk. "Here is the report on the Shenandoah power project—just came in. And Talbot and Davis would like your approval of the Harrisburg traction merger."

"Ah, yes. Very good. And how is everything otherwise, Roder?"

"Going very nicely, sir. Although I regret to say that Miss McNeill is not here today.

Her sister telephoned that she had met with an accident. In fact, according to the newspaper, she has been the victim of a cowardly assault."

"What? Why—"

Mr. Ogden's voice quivered with anxiety. He rose from his chair and seized the newspaper.

"Mysterious Invader Attacks Girl in Apartment," he read. Then followed an account of the outrage, written in lurid style:

Miss Margaret McNeill, who lived with her sister, Mrs. Sommers, on Eighty-second Street, had been spending the day with friends at Stamford. On her return, about 11 o'clock at night, she entered the apartment, to be confronted by a masked bandit, who, taking advantage of the tenants' absence, had ransacked the place.

The masked man, after tearing Miss McNeill's clothes off her in a mysterious and frantic search, had proceeded to beat her cruelly, injuring her arm and side to such an extent that she had to be taken to the hospital.

The injured girl could not be seen last night, but it was learned from her sister, Mrs. Sommers, that a hasty examination of the apartment indicated that nothing had been stolen.

Mrs. Sommers could imagine no reason for the masked man's presence or for his attack upon her sister. The whole affair seemed shrouded in mystery. Miss McNeill, who was in the employ of Mr. William Ogden, the well known financier, with offices in the Union Trust Building, was a young woman of unusual beauty and charm. And so on.

Mr. Ogden, having finished reading the article, stood staring at the paper before him. Mr. Roder shifted from one foot to the other. A heavy silence lay upon the room. The blood rose in Mr. Ogden's neck, his cheeks.

"What do you make of it, Roder?" he asked.

"A mistake, I should think. The man probably got into the wrong apartment."

"Perhaps," Mr. Ogden said, but made no further comment. "That's all, at present, Roder," he added.

When Mr. Roder had gone, Mr. Ogden departed. Finding a taxicab, he directed the chauffeur to take him to the Roosevelt Hospital. A dreadful suspicion had been growing in his mind—a suspicion that, by now, had become almost a certainty. The masked man had been after his letters—the letters he had written to Honey from Paris.

LOVE'S GREATEST MISTAKE 185

How anyone could have known of their existence, except through Honey, he could not imagine. Of course the girl might have been indiscreet enough to talk, but surely to no one but her sister.

He tried to remember precisely what he had said, realizing that, whatever it was, it could be used against him by anyone sufficiently unscrupulous to resort to blackmail. Had the thief, after his attack on Honey, obtained possession of the letters? Only Honey could tell him that.

Two men were standing near the entrance as he reached it. Mr. Ogden was far too agitated to notice them. Had he done so, he might have recognized in one the sleek person of Mr. Ray Becker. The other was a reporter from a sensational newspaper.

When word came to Honey of Mr. Ogden's arrival she was talking to Jane about the latter's trip to Long Beach the night before. Her body was rigid with bandages and plaster.

"Was Ray Becker with you?" she asked.

"No. He had an engagement."

Honey sighed. Her sister's answer told her what she wanted to know. It had been Ray who had attacked her. And Mona had arranged a clear field for him.

186 LOVE'S GREATEST MISTAKE

She felt a dreadful bitterness. These crooks had pretended to be her friends. Had she any real friends? What was the use? All these people had a certain cynical philosophy: to get what they could out of life, no matter what the cost. She was glad to be rid of them.

When she saw Mr. Ogden coming toward her, she had a feeling of comfort, of warmth. He had never doubted her. In her suffering, her weariness of spirit, she turned to him with a smile. Here was one man, at least, upon whose friendship, whose love, she could depend. She put out her free hand. He would kiss her, no doubt, in spite of Jane's presence.

Mr. Ogden, however, had experienced a great shock. Love—secret love—was one thing; the pitiless opinion of the world quite another. The article in the newspaper had filled him with dreadful fears. He did not even see Honey's outstretched hand.

"My letters," he said curtly. "Did they get them?"

Honey shivered. She had risked her life on this man's account!

In that moment her faith in love—in life itself—was swept away. She lay staring up at him, very still and small and cold.

CHAPTER XXI

When Honey, lying on a cot in one of the public wards at Roosevelt Hospital, saw Mr. Ogden coming toward her, she almost forgot her pain. Here was one man, at least, who trusted her—believed in her. Loved her, too, as his letters had shown. She would have held out both arms to him, had her bandages permitted. As it was, one lay extended, white and slim, toward him—and he did not notice it. He did not ask about her injuries; he did not stoop to kiss her.

"My letters!" he exclaimed. "Did they get them?"

Honey shivered as if a harsh wind had suddenly swept over her. Life was a cruel affair, but she was learning something.

"No," she answered wearily.

Mr. Ogden smiled for the first time since he had read the article in the newspaper.

"Where are they?" he asked.

Honey did not answer him at first. When

she finally spoke, it was slowly, deliberately, her voice flat and colorless.

"I have them. Unfortunately, I told certain persons—friends, I thought—that you had written to me. They wanted me to join them in an attempt to get money from you—blackmail you. I should never have trusted them, in the first place. It was a mistake. When I found out what they were after, I hid the letters where no one would find them.

"The man who ransacked the apartment last night tried to make me tell him where they were. I refused. Then he hurt me. That's the whole story.

"Jane"—she turned to her sister—"this is Mr. Ogden. I believe you two have never met. Hand me my silver mirror, will you, dear?—the one I asked you to bring down this morning?"

She turned again to Mr. Ogden.

"You see," she smiled, "I read a story, once, about a woman hiding valuable papers in the back of a picture frame, and so I thought a mirror would be as good a place—even better. Under the glass, Jane. First you have to take out the ring."

When her sister had done as she directed,

LOVE'S GREATEST MISTAKE 189

Honey lifted from the hollow metal back of the mirror the three letters Mr. Ogden had written her.

"Here," she said, and handed them to him.

He gave them a quick, satisfied glance, then thrust them into his pocket. Only then did he show any appreciation of what Honey had risked to safeguard his name, his reputation. As far as she was concerned, his appreciation came too late.

"Dear child!" he exclaimed, pressing her unresponsive hand. "You—you've been wonderful, to do what you have for me. Wonderful! Are you much hurt?"

"Two broken ribs and a dislocated shoulder, to start with," Jane said acidly. "The doctors haven't decided what else. They've taken X-ray pictures. We're waiting to hear."

Mr. Ogden's eyes, filled with contrition, sought Honey's. As his fear of public scandal receded, his desire for Honey came flooding back. How fragile, how lovely, she looked lying against the pillows! She was almost as white as they—except for her gay mop of hair.

Only now did he seem to realize that she was in a public ward—that there were rows and rows of other sufferers in the pain-laden room. He took up his hat, very eager, very solicitous.

"I'll see that you have a private room at once," he whispered. "And a night and a day nurse—the best medical attention in New York. It isn't much, I know, in return for all you've done; but it's the best I can offer at the moment. Later on—"

His eyes, meeting Honey's, spoke of other, more important things—of the proposal he had made to her on the eve of his sailing, to which, so far, she had given him no answer.

"Jane," Honey said, "would you mind leaving us for a moment? There is something I want to talk to Mr. Ogden about—privately."

"Of course," Jane hurried out.

When they were alone, Honey motioned Mr. Ogden to the side of her bed.

"When you went away," she whispered, her eyes very calm and grave, "you asked me to become your mistress."

In spite of his quick gesture of protest she went on:

"You did not call it that, but it meant the same thing. You offered me a lot of money— an income for life, I believe—if I would live with you. That is true, isn't it?"

"Why, yes—in a sense—if you choose to put it that way. I wanted you—still want you—as a man might want a wife—honestly, sincerely, because I love you. I'd have asked you to marry me if I were free. I think you know that."

"I don't know it, Mr. Ogden," Honey said quickly. "I don't believe it. When you went away I did—but not now. You knew when you came here that I had been hurt—badly enough hurt to be in a hospital. You must have guessed why—your first question told me that. Yet you were so frightened by fear of publicity—of what people might say—that you had only one thought in mind—your own safety. Mine came second. You did not ask me how I felt, how badly I was hurt. You asked about your letters.

"If you had loved me—really loved me—you would never have done that. You would have thought of me first—have forgotten everything in your anxiety over my condition. I don't know what answer I might have made to you if you had taken me in your arms, kissed me, the moment you got here. I've been fond of you—very fond. And I've been hungry for love, too—real love. Sometimes I think there isn't any such thing. I don't know. But I do know this—I haven't found it yet.

"No"—rather wearily she resisted his attempt to embrace, to kiss her—"it's no use—now. Let's be friends—if we can. We'll never be anything more."

Mr. Ogden made no effort to argue with her. In his heart he knew that she spoke the truth.

"And you?" he asked gravely. "What are you going to do?"

"I don't know. Work, of course. But not for you. After what has happened, I couldn't. Since I came to New York I've dreamed of money, of luxury, of the easiest way. My sister, my so-called friends, everyone—even you, Mr. Ogden—have preached money to me: told me that, with my good looks, I could get anything I wanted.

"That isn't true. I want love, and you can't buy that. A fortune-teller once predicted that I was going to marry a millionaire, and I was fool enough to believe it. I've been a fool in lots of ways, I guess. But—I'm learning."

With a queer, wistful smile, she put out her hand.

"Good-by. You'd better go now. I'm tired."

When he had left her, she began to cry very softly, without knowing just why.

CHAPTER XXII

HAVING, on the impulse of the moment, given orders that Honey was to be moved to the finest private room in the hospital, with a day and a night nurse in attendance, and having further insisted that his own physician, one of the best in New York, should be consulted regarding her case, Mr. Ogden ate a hurried luncheon and went back to his office.

Here, over his engineering reports, his traction mergers, he became again the serious business man. His desire for Honey remained; but perhaps he recognized, in the rather bitter things she had said to him, a basis of truth.

Not even for Honey's white and gold and scarlet self would he be willing to have his letters to her made public. He knew how the world would laugh. And he was very fond of his wife. The thought of humiliating her in any way pained him. Then, too, the hot, reckless blood of youth was lacking—the divine folly that is the very essence of love.

Well, perhaps it was better, he reflected,

LOVE'S GREATEST MISTAKE

to go on pleasantly, comfortably, making money, spending it, playing with his racing stable, his Japanese prints. Safe playthings, if not very exciting ones. That was what age meant—safety. Honey was right. He did not really love her—as youth desires to be loved.

But admitting the fact did not lessen Mr. Ogden's hurt. He had cared for Honey sincerely, deeply, and he had lost her. When his secretary came in with a card, he looked up, frowning.

The card was that of Mr. Ray Becker. It bore a penciled message explaining that Mr. Becker was the friend of Miss McNeill's whom Mr. Ogden had met at the Red Peacock. Following was the word "Important," heavily underlined. Mr. Ogden's frown deepened.

"I'll see him," he said, wondering what the man might want—afraid to send him away without finding out.

Mr. Becker strode into the private office, a cold smile along his thin, hard lip. He took the chair toward which Mr. Ogden nodded, and before speaking paused to light a cigarette. Mr. Ogden meanwhile studied him through narrowed eyes. "Dangerous," he thought, and waited.

"I came," Mr. Becker presently said, his voice very cool and level, "to ask your advice about a matter that concerns Miss McNeill."

"Well?" Mr. Ogden questioned, a bit impatiently.

"You know, of course, that she was attacked in her sister's apartment last night by a masked man whose purpose in going there was not clear. 'Shrouded in mystery,' I think one of the papers put it." He named a sensational sheet.

This time Mr. Ogden merely nodded grimly.

"The newspapers," Mr. Becker went on, "are naturally eager to learn the truth about the affair. They smell a big scandal—something not apparent on the surface. I think, from what I can gather, that Miss McNeill has been going about with you—"

Mr. Ogden's self-control broke. He brought his fist down violently upon the top of his desk.

"Are you trying to blackmail me?" he exclaimed.

"I'm trying to tell you something, Mr. Ogden," Mr. Becker said coolly, "that I think you ought to know. I am a friend of Miss McNeill's, and I don't want to see her reputation injured.

"I can't help it if the city editor of one of New York's biggest dailies scents a scandal. I can't help it if he assigns to the case a reporter who has the reputation of never failing to dig up the truth. But it happens that this reporter is an acquaintance of mine. He came to me at once because he thought that, being a friend of Miss McNeill's, I might give him some information.

"He showed me the story he's going to turn in for the morning edition. It suggests that the masked man might have been in search of letters written to Miss McNeill by a well known New York financier, and that she risked her life to save his reputation.

"It also contains a statement that the financier in question, on learning of Miss McNeill's condition, at once hastened to the hospital to see her, as well as to make arrangements for a private room, nurses, the services of his own high-priced physician. The orders at the hospital were given openly enough. The gentleman in question made no attempt to conceal his identity.

"It is also a matter of common knowledge that Miss McNeill has for some time past been employed by that gentleman in his office. She has been seen with him in restaurants, night clubs, at the theater.

"My reporter friend thinks he has a very interesting story. He will state only facts, of course. But, while Miss McNeill has herself declined to make any explanation of the attack upon her, one of the nurses in the ward distinctly heard Miss McNeill's wealthy friend, when he called upon her this morning, ask if they had got his letters."

Mr. Ogden did not move, but there was rage in his eyes. Mr. Becker, seeing it, swung his right arm across his chest so that his fingers, beneath the lapel of his coat, touched the automatic pistol slung under his left arm. Mr. Ogden saw the movement and understood it.

"To me," Mr. Becker went on smoothly, "all this seems a great pity. I begged my friend not to turn in such a story. He laughed and said people might think, of course, that she and the financier in question had been—well —more than just—friends; but that his paper demanded the truth, and printed it—that if people did indiscreet things it wasn't his fault. His employers believed in publicity, no matter whom it hurt."

Mr. Ogden's face had grown a trifle pale,

but his jaws were firmly set. It was not the first time he had faced a blackmailer.

"I suppose," he sneered, "that your newspaper friend—if indeed you have any such friend—would be willing to tear up the story for a consideration."

"I think he might," Mr. Becker assented, "although when I first mentioned it to him he became very angry. But I happen to know he has a wife and two children, to say nothing of a leaky heart, and that it has been the dream of his life to buy a place up the Sound somewhere and settle down to the life of a country gentleman. So when I spoke of a couple of hundred thousand dollars—"

Mr. Ogden rose in his chair, his shoulders as straight as they had been in France ten years before.

"Get out!" he said. "Publish what you damn please. If you libel me I'll sue."

Mr. Becker, who had also risen, made another attempt.

"It is possible that a hundred and fifty thousand," he said, "might appeal to him."

"Not a cent!"

"Very well. The story goes in. Your name as the author of the letters will be omitted, of course—to make the public eager for more details. I may be able to supply some myself, and so may Miss Terry, who read your letters. Even Miss McNeill may be induced to speak."

He took up his hat.

"If you want to see me tonight or tomorrow, my address and telephone number are on my card."

"Get out of my office!" Mr. Ogden thundered.

Thank God, this scoundrel had not succeeded in getting hold of the letters themselves. Taking them from his pocket, Mr. Ogden tore them to shreds, then carefully burned the fragments in the open fireplace that decorated one end of his office.

Ray Becker's story of a friend on one of the newspapers was true enough up to the point that the friend was ready to "sell out" for money. That was pure fiction. Any money Mr. Becker hoped to extract from Mr. Ogden would be for his own personal benefit. But his friend did want news, and Mr. Becker hurried downtown to give it to him. Mr. Ogden, he decided, needed to be thoroughly scared.

CHAPTER XXIII

Honey had other visitors, that first day at the hospital, in addition to Mr. Ogden.

For one, there was Herbert Gibbs. He came in just after luncheon, and stood for a moment at Honey's bedside, gazing down at her drawn face.

"How are you feeling, dear?" he whispered, touching her hand softly.

"Lots of pain." She looked up with a wistful smile.

"I'd have come before if I had known. I only learned of your—trouble—when one of our men called my attention to the article in the newspaper."

He glanced around the private room to which Honey had been moved an hour before.

"They sent me to the public wards at first," said Honey. "This is better."

"Yes."

For a moment Honey almost hated him. Anyone would know she could not afford such accommodations. Why not tell him the truth?

In her disillusionment with life, Honey longed more and more for frankness, for honesty.

"Mr. Ogden got the room for me," she said. "He's a very rich—a very prosperous—man. And, of course, I am one of his employees."

Herbert Gibbs' brows drew into a quick frown. He said nothing, but his eyes held many questions.

Should she go on? Honey asked herself. She wanted to, but somehow could not. She remembered that Herbert had once warned her against Mr. Ogden; against accepting his attentions. She remained silent.

"I've sent some flowers," he said presently.

"That was mighty sweet of you," Honey told him, rebellion in her heart.

What right had he to judge her, unheard? Then she realized that he had not judged her at all—that she, in fact, was judging him.

"Have they found out anything more about the man who—attacked you?" he was asking.

She shook her head without speaking.

"Oh, well"—he dismissed the matter with a gesture—"you shouldn't be bothered about such things now. Not about anything. But don't forget"—he pressed her hand with quick tenderness—"that I've asked you a question and am waiting for your answer to it."

Sudden tears sprang to Honey's eyes. So she had misjudged him, after all. For a moment her fingers clung to his.

"You gave me a week, remember," she said, smiling through her tears. "Before I *do* answer you, Herbert, there's something I must explain. I don't feel equal to it now."

She made up her mind, in that instant, to tell him everything that had occurred between Mr. Ogden and herself. After all, there was nothing so serious about it. Then, if he still wanted her—

"That's right," he laughed. "I *did* give you a week. My own suggestion, too. But you don't have to take it unless you want to."

Her beauty, as she lay there, had driven all doubts of her from his mind. She was so utterly lovely and adorable.

"Why not tell me tomorrow?" he whispered, again pressing her hand. "It will take only one word. If it's the right one, I'll be the happiest man this side of Paradise."

"Very well," Honey said slowly. "I'll tell you tomorrow. Everything." Herbert bent and kissed her tenderly on the lips.

When he had gone, Honey lay smiling against

her pillows. The things that Mona Terry, that Ray Becker, that Mr. Ogden had done to her had hurt—bitterly. But Herbert trusted her, believed in her. She would tell him all, tomorrow. She wanted his respect, at least.

As for marrying him—she stared up at the ceiling, tracing interminably a tiny crack in the plaster. Why had Don Kendall not been to see her? She had expected him all day. Surely he had forgotten their little quarrel.

Then, without warning, he came, shouldering his way impetuously past the nurses, the interne at the door—strode into the room, carrying a great bunch of roses in his hands.

"Hello, Hon!" he cried, giving the flowers to the nurse. "Guess you've been wondering why I didn't come around before. Don't worry. I telephoned—found out all about you; how you were getting along and everything. Dad had me on the carpet this morning. Said I was spending too much money and ought to go to work. Said I ought to get married, too. What do you think of that?"

He sat down at Honey's side, laughing so heartily that she could not help joining him, although in her heart she saw nothing ludicrous in the idea of his getting married.

"I'm awfully glad to see you, Don," she said.

"Glad to see you, Honey darlin'. Don't you know I love you? Am crazy about you? Always have been. But, as I told dad, this marriage business isn't in my line. How do you feel, now that the sawbones have got through with you?"

"Like a—a mummy," Honey laughed. "All bound around with plaster and adhesive tape. I can scarcely breathe."

Don patted her small hand with his huge paw.

"I never did have a chance to tell you, last night, how I happened in," he laughed. "I'd been up in Canada—fishing. Couldn't seem to concentrate on it, somehow, thinking about you. So I packed my kit and came back to town. Say, how long do you think you'll have to stay in this hospital, Honey child?"

"A month, maybe," Honey told him.

"No! You don't mean it. Well, in that case I might as well go back to camp—till you get well, you know. They tell me you're not in any danger. Or, instead of fishing, I might take a run down to Barbados. That's dad's big idea."

"Barbados? What for?" Honey's heart sank.

"Oh—something about his steamship lines. Agent down there has gone to the bad—whole office in a jam."

"Are you going?" Honey asked.

"Well—that's the question. What I wanted to do was play around New York for a while with you. That's out, now, for a month at least."

"I think you ought to go," Honey said.

"Why?"

"Because—because your father wants you to, I suppose. And, after all, he's your father."

Don looked at Honey with new interest.

"Say—do you know," he laughed, "there's something in that. Hanged if I don't do it, now that *you're* lost to me for a month. Only" —he laughed again—"I'll have to get up tomorrow morning about the time I usually go to bed. One of the old man's steamers, the *Buenos Aires,* sails early in the morning. He wants me to take her. I'm to let him know tonight.

"Look here, Honey: Promise me you won't forget all about me while I'm gone, and I'll do it. I'm sick of New York, anyway. What do you say?"

"I—I promise I won't forget you," Honey whispered, her voice trembling. "Oh, Don," she murmured to herself, "if only you would take me in your arms and—"

As though in answer to her wish, he bent down and gave her a long, soul-stirring kiss.

"You're such a darlin', Honey girl," he whispered, his lips against hers. "Such a perfect darlin'! God knows, I'm going to miss you. But when I come back"—he kissed her again—"we'll have some wonderful times together. Wonderful!"

Then the nurse tapped on the door, and Don left, promising Honey he would write.

CHAPTER XXIV

When Lovey Gibbs appeared at the table next morning, the rest of the family had very nearly finished their meal. Herbert, thinking of Honey, was planning to take an early train to the city. While waiting for her coffee to be brought in, Lovey began to glance through her favorite newspaper.

Suddenly a headline caught the girl's eye.

"Mystery in Attack on Girl Deepens," she read. "Compromising Letters from Millionaire Believed Cause of Outrage." Then followed the main body of the story. Lovey, who doted on sensation and mystery, proceeded to read the article aloud:

The man who brutally attacked a young and beautiful stenographer in her Eighty-second Street apartment Wednesday night, and injured her so badly that she is now in Roosevelt Hospital, has not yet been located by the police; but certain very interesting facts have come to hand which may throw some light upon what is now an unsolved mystery.

There is reason to believe that the masked man who first ransacked the apartment which Miss McNeill shared with her sister, and then subjected the former to a beating which resulted in the dislocation of her shoulder and the fracture of two ribs, was no ordinary sneak thief or burglar.

On the contrary, it is thought by the police that the man visited the apartment in search of certain letters, said to have been written to Miss McNeill by a prominent and extremely wealthy New Yorker with whom she has been seen of late in some of the smart night clubs of the city.

"Well—what do you think of that?" Lovey exclaimed, grinning over the top of the newspaper.

A ghastly silence fell upon the breakfast table. Lovey had completely forgotten that Honey's last name was McNeill, and Herbert had not mentioned the girl's unfortunate experience because he feared his mother might not understand it.

Gazing across the table, Lovey saw her brother attempt to put down his coffee cup—heard it crash to the floor.

Mrs. Gibbs and Josephine were staring at him, wide-eyed.

"Why, you people—what on earth's the matter?" Lovey cried.

"I'm not surprised," Josephine said coldly. "A kept woman."

"It's a lie!"

Herbert reached across the table and tore the newspaper from his sister's grasp. But when he had glanced through the article he sank back in his chair as if he had received a deathblow.

"Herbert!" Lovey gasped, understanding at last. "I—I didn't know it was—Honey! Honest, I didn't! I'm so sorry!"

Herbert said nothing. His face had grown suddenly gray, old.

Don Kendall left the hospital, after his talk with Honey, rather glad than otherwise that he had decided to go to Barbados. He had not told Honey all that his father had said to him that morning. Mr. Kendall, Senior, had been rather positive. Stories had reached him to the effect that Don was being seen too frequently in the night clubs—was squandering his money and, what was more important, his health, too lavishly along upper Broadway. The tangle in the agent's office at Barbados was not particularly serious. Only a strong and positive hand was needed to straighten matters out; and the man Mr. Kendall would otherwise have sent was in the hospital, recovering from an attack of appendicitis.

It seemed to Mr. Kendall an excellent opportunity for Don. He had therefore stated, with his accustomed positiveness, that, unless Don *did* go, his allowance would be cut in half.

At first Don decided to make a big night of it and to board the steamer at dawn. But when he had packed his things and sent them to the boat, he changed his mind. There were so many girls—women—with whom he was in the habit of amusing himself. A big party had already been arranged for the evening, to celebrate in proper fashion his return to New York. Why should visions of Honey, in her high hospital bed, cause him to hesitate—to think that the party would be a bore? Was he falling in love? Absurd! Don had decided long ago that love—marriage—were synonymous with death: the death of joy, of freedom, of life as he intended to live it. Thoughts of Honey brought other things to mind—things to which he had so far given but small attention. Why had she been attacked so viciously? Who was the man with the hard eyes, the sleek black hair, that he had seen coming out of the apartment—the supposed burglar who had attacked her?

This was a matter to be looked into, Barbados or no Barbados. One person might know the truth—Jane Sommers. On impulse, he called her up.

"Hello, Jane," he said. "This is Don Kendall. I want to see you for a few minutes. Right away. May I come now?"

"Why—yes," Jane told him, wondering what had happened to make his voice so stern.

She was still wondering when Don strode into the living-room—was hoping he might have come to see *her*.

His first words dispelled any such idea.

"It's about Honey," he said. "I've just remembered that I saw the man I met coming out of here, last night, at the Paradise Club one evening. Dining with your sister and two other people. I thought you might know who he is—why he came? You didn't seem to, last night."

Jane sat for a moment in silence. When she spoke, there were new lights in her eyes.

"Don," she said, "Honey came to New York a good girl. She's a good girl now. But this town has hurt her a lot. Maybe I've hurt her,

LOVE'S GREATEST MISTAKE 213

too. Not that I've done anything wrong," she hastened to add. "But I've allowed her to go around with the wrong people—to get wrong ideas about money—about life in general. I did ask you to let her alone, but—I should have done more.

"That man you saw coming out of here last night is a crook, a blackmailer. His name is Ray Becker. Honey met him through a girl from our home town—Mona Terry. This fellow Becker has Mona under his thumb. She's crazy about him, of course.

"Mr. Ogden, in whose office Honey worked, fell in love with her. Offered her a lot of money to—well, you know. While he was abroad last month, he wrote Honey a couple of sentimental letters. Becker wanted them, so he could blackmail Ogden. Honey let herself be beaten up, rather than tell where they were.

"That's the sort of girl she is, Don, and I'm proud of her. And if you are the sort of man I think you are, you'll let her alone, as I've asked you to before. There's one man in her life who really cares for her—wants to marry her—Herbert Gibbs. *You* only want to be amused. Why not give her a chance?"

Don, who still was standing in the middle of the room, straightened his shoulders.

"I'll give her all the chance she wants," he said grimly. "What do you think I am, anyway? I'm sailing for the West Indies early tomorrow morning. Going aboard the steamer tonight, in fact. But, before I go, there's a little matter I want to attend to—a little matter with this fellow Becker. You say he's trying to blackmail Ogden?"

"Yes. He hoped to do it with the letters. Since he didn't get them, he may try other means. By threatening publicity, perhaps. Ray Becker is a very dangerous man."

Don stood very still, his clenched fists straining at the linings of his coat pockets.

"Where can I find Becker?" he asked.

"I don't know. But I can give you the address of Mona Terry, who's been working with him."

Jane looked up the number of Mona's apartment in the telephone directory, scribbled it on a card.

"Thanks." Don thrust the card into his pocket and put out his hand. "You've been a good pal, Jane. Good-by. I won't see you again. And I won't bother Honey any more, either. I'm glad she has a chance to marry someone who cares for her. Only—promise me one thing: Don't tell her about this talk we've had, will you? Just let her think I've—forgotten all about her."

When he had gone, Jane leaned for many minutes against the closed door, crying bitterly.

CHAPTER XXV

Ray Becker, having supplied his newspaper friend with sufficient information to "throw a scare" into Mr. Ogden, proceeded uptown for a talk with Mona Terry.

He needed more evidence, stronger proof, before he interviewed Ogden again: proof that the letters actually had been written. Only one person could provide that proof—Mona Terry. She had read them—was in a position to testify concerning their contents. Once Mona had given him a sworn statement—He chuckled at the thought of placing a document of that nature beneath Mr. Ogden's nose.

He found Mona in a black humor, caused in part by remorse because of the harm she had done to Honey. This, however, Mr. Becker might have overcome, as he had overcome it in the past, by his hold upon the girl—her infatuation for him.

But there was another reason for Mona's ill temper: A man she knew, eager to supplant Ray in her affections, had come to her with the

LOVE'S GREATEST MISTAKE

report that Ray had boasted openly, in the Red Peacock the night before, that as soon as he made his "clean-up" he was going to Paris, taking with him one Gwen Joyce, who danced in the cabaret there. Asked concerning Mona, he had coolly announced that he intended to "give that dumb Dora the air."

"Help you collect a bunch of jack, so you can take that Joyce girl to Europe?" she cried, when Ray spoke of the sworn statement. "Tell me a really funny story. That one's cold."

"Somebody's been filling you up with a lot of bunk," Ray said, and tried to win her with kisses.

But Mona pushed him away.

"You've kidded me long enough," she wept. "I'm through! I'll sign nothing to get Honey McNeill into any more trouble. "Ray"—she made a last tearful appeal—"forget this blackmail stuff and marry me. You know I'm crazy about you. I'll work for you—anything—if you'll only go straight."

Mr. Becker's look of amazement changed to anger.

"Marry you!" he sneered. "Tell *me* a funny story! What do you take me for—a simp?"

218 LOVE'S GREATEST MISTAKE

"I'll go to the police!" Mona screamed. "I'll give them the low-down. I'll see whether that dirty little alley cat, Gwen Joyce, can come between—"

Then Ray struck her. She went down, a crumpled, ungainly heap, across the floor.

Without troubling to find out whether she was alive or dead, Mr. Becker opened the door of the apartment—opened it, unluckily for him, to find Don Kendall in the very act of ringing the bell.

"Who do you want?" Ray asked, trying to force his way out.

"You," Don said quietly, and stiff-armed Mr. Ray Becker right back into the living-room.

The door swung to behind them. As Ray's fingers closed on the stock of his automatic, Don's almost crushed his wrist.

"So that's it, you rat!" Don exclaimed, tossing the pistol across the room. With almost the same movement, he flung Mr. Becker into a chair.

Mona, creeping to her feet, a smear of blood across her cheek, faced them.

"I wouldn't care if you killed him!" she cried. "He—he almost killed me."

LOVE'S GREATEST MISTAKE

"You're Mona Terry, I suppose," Don said.

"Yes. And I want you to know that I'm through—through with him and his blackmailing schemes."

"You're through, all right," Don said. "Don't worry about that. And so is he. I saw him coming out of Jane Sommers' apartment last night, and I could turn him over to the police if I wanted to. But that wouldn't be so good. Might cause trouble for Honey. Get her name in the papers. I've got a better plan than that. I'm going to put him to work —give him a chance to earn an honest dollar. I imagine it will be a new experience."

"What's that?" Mr. Becker cried, springing to his feet. "You can't make me do anything, you big bluff!"

"Think so? Well, my lad, I'm going to put you to work in the stokehold of a nice little ocean-going steamer bound for the Argentine Republic. That's easy for me, since my old man happens to own the boat!"

"The hell you say!"

In his fury, Mr. Becker launched a right-hand swing and caught Don on the jaw. It was, for him, a most unfortunate blow. Don Kendall had been merely waiting for an excuse.

"It's coming to you, I guess," he said, and led swiftly with his left.

Even Mona Terry, when asked about it afterward, could not speak of the encounter as a fight. A massacre, she described it. With less than a dozen blows Mr. Becker was reduced to a mass of gibbering pulp.

"Wash the blood off his face," Don commanded. "Straighten him up a bit, so I can take him to my cab. And listen, you"— He stood for a moment over Mr. Becker's crumpled figure. "If I ever catch you in New York again, or hear of your saying anything against Miss McNeill, I'll kill you. Do you understand that?"

It was perhaps fortunate that Don Kendall, as he glanced through the newspapers off Sandy Hook the next morning, did not happen to read the particular paper that contained the sensational article about Honey McNeill. Otherwise Mr. Ray Becker, sweating in the stokehold below, would doubtless have suffered an even more dreadful fate. Which is saying a great deal, as that young man was going through about all he could stand.

CHAPTER XXVI

Honey read the article about herself while eating breakfast. The day nurse, very excited, had brought the paper in.

"Is it true, Miss McNeill?" she asked. "About the letters? If it is, and you wouldn't tell, I think you are just about the bravest woman I know!"

To Honey this aspect of the case was a new one. She had read the story, covered with shame, because of the relations between Mr. Ogden and herself which it so plainly implied.

"I'm afraid that won't help me any," she said, with a smile that was almost humorous. "It isn't my bravery people are going to talk about now. It's my morals. But I can tell you better," Honey added, "when I've seen the man who wants to marry me. He asked me yesterday to give him my answer today. Maybe I won't have to give him any now." She tried to smile. "But I still think he'll come."

Herbert did come, driving to the hospital

the moment he reached New York. Stern, silent, he stood beside her bed.

"Honey," he said, "is all this true?"

"Sit down, please," Honey whispered, patting the side of the bed.

But Herbert took a chair. The nurse had already disappeared.

"I'm going to tell you everything," Honey went on. "I would have, anyway, even if this story had not come out. That was why I wouldn't give you my answer yesterday. I wanted you to know the truth, first. And yesterday I was too tired to tell it to you."

She was very lovely in her pallor. Her large eyes glowed feverishly against the whiteness of her cheeks. Herbert Gibbs felt a desire to sweep her into his arms, to comfort her with kisses.

"That's all I ask," he said quickly. "The truth. All I've ever asked, Honey. I'm not accusing you."

"Yes, you are, Herbert. I can see it in your eyes. Well, you may be right. There *were* letters—three of them—written to me by Mr. Ogden while he was abroad, in Paris. I wish I had them to show you; but I gave them back to him yesterday.

"The man who attacked me tried to force me to give him the letters. He wanted to use them in blackmailing Mr. Ogden. There were things in them—about how much Mr. Ogden cared for me—that might have made him a great deal of trouble with his wife. Yes, he's married. I thought you knew that. His wife is abroad.

"Of course I had no right to go around with him—to encourage him. That was my mistake. I thought he was just a pleasant friend. Later on he said he loved me—would marry me if he were free. I don't know whether he would or not. He wanted me to live with him—and offered me a great deal of money if I would. I was to think the matter over and let him know my decision on his return from abroad."

In her anger, her pride, Honey spared herself no single detail, glossed over no slightest fact.

"I liked him—a lot. If I hadn't I don't suppose I'd have gone around with him—or let myself be hurt, the way I was, on his account. He's paying for this room, the doctors, the nurses, because of that.

"Of course you wouldn't want to marry me

now. You couldn't. Everybody will think I'm just—rotten, crooked, a gold-digger. Why shouldn't they? I can imagine just what your mother and sisters will say. I'm ruined, as far as my reputation is concerned, whether I've done anything to deserve it or not. So, you see—"

She paused, hoping pitifully that he would understand—would laugh, perhaps, and tell her that to him the world's opinion made no possible difference; that he believed in her, loved her, as before.

"I don't care anything about letters—such things," he said sternly. "Although I should have thought, when that old rotter Ogden asked you to be his"—looking at Honey's white face, he could not bring himself to utter the word—"when he asked you to live with him, you would have slapped his face. The only question I want to ask is, was there anything wrong—ever—between you two?"

He faltered as he asked the question, and seemed just a trifle ashamed of it.

Honey stared at him, her eyes burning. Then, with a sigh, she sank back against the pillows.

"If you loved me, Herbert," she said softly

LOVE'S GREATEST MISTAKE 225

—"if you really and truly loved me, you would never have asked me that question."

"But—why not? Don't you see it's the one question I've got to ask—the one thing that really matters? All you need do is tell me there was never anything wrong between Mr. Ogden and you, and I'll believe you."

"No, you won't, Herbert. You might pretend to, but you wouldn't really. If you've doubted me once you'll always doubt me, no matter what I say."

Like all the rest, Herbert had failed her. Love! There was no such thing, so far as men were concerned. Only passion—desire. She knew that even now, had she cared to do so, she could have swayed him by a physical appeal —knew that he was hungry to put his arms around her and kiss her.

"You'd better run along now, Herbert," she said. "I couldn't marry you, anyway, after what's happened, no matter whether I'm a 'good' woman or a bad one. It would separate you from your family, ruin your business career—your whole life. Don't you see that, whether my virtue is gone or not, my reputation is—which is what really counts with the world? I've committed the unpardonable sin of being found out. It's too bad, of course, but the only thing you can do now is forget me. I'm finished—done for!"

Honey turned her face from him, buried it in the pillows.

Even yet, Herbert might have saved the situation but for his hard puritanical pride—a pride of family, of name.

"You know I love you, Honey," he said. "But I've got to trust you, too. You can't expect me to do that without perfect confidence between us. I'd rather have the truth from you, whatever it is, than nothing at all. When you are ready to answer my question, let me know." Trembling a little he turned from her, walked out of the room.

When Jane arrived, an hour later, she noticed that her sister's pillow was wet with tears, and that a newspaper lay on Honey's bed.

"It's a rotten shame!" she said. "I should think you could sue for damages."

"Why? They didn't say a thing that wasn't true."

"They implied a lot, which is worse. Think what mother—the people at home—will say. Some kind friend is sure to mail them the clipping. Why—they'll call you terrible things. A gold-digger! A kept woman! It's fierce!"

"I guess they will," Honey said wearily.

"I wonder how Mr. Gibbs will take it," Jane went on. "Have you heard from him?"

"Yes. He was here an hour ago, on his way to the office."

"What did he say?"

"He asked me," Honey replied, with a scornful laugh, "if I was a 'good' woman."

"Well—you could tell him you were, I hope?"

"Tell him! Good Lord, Jane—would I have to *tell* him that? Would I have to tell *you?* Don't you *know?*"

Jane Sommers sat silent for some minutes, a curious expression on her face.

"From what I've seen of life, Honey," she said presently, "I've come to the conclusion that goodness in a woman, or lack of it, is almost entirely a question of how far she has been tempted."

CHAPTER XXVII

Honey's injuries—her physical ones—mended quickly. Mentally she did not mend at all. It is not well for youth to be introspective. The girl lay on her cot, alone, hour after hour, day after day, thinking—thinking—thinking.

Except for Jane, she had no callers now. Mr. Ogden came no more.

Mr. Roder appeared one day with a verbal message from his employer. Honey was to stay on at the hospital as long as necessary. Her bills would be paid. She was not to worry. In an envelope that Mr. Roder handed her was a letter of recommendation. There was also a month's salary.

Of Mona, of Ray Becker, she heard nothing, which caused her no regret. She had finished with such reptiles, she hoped.

As the days lengthened into weeks, with no word from Don Kendall, Honey's melancholia increased. He had promised to write; he had

A Paramount Picture. *Love's Greatest Mistake.*
HARVEY SWALLOWS HIS PRIDE AND COMES TO SEE THE
WOUNDED HONEY.

not done so. Jane, who could have supplied the reason, remained silent.

Nor did Honey hear anything from Herbert Gibbs. But that caused her no surprise. She pictured him working over his drawings, nursing his hurt pride, listening daily, no doubt, to lectures from his mother on the virtues of the Gibbs family name.

Jane sat with her daily, and once brought George, who was spending the week-end in town. It pleased Honey to see that Jane was paying more attention to her husband, making much of him.

Shortly before she left the hospital, she received a cruelly bitter letter from her brother Martin, saying that he had read of her disgrace in the New York papers; that he had kept the matter from his mother—as if the poor soul were not Honey's mother. He "washed his hands of her," he concluded his letter, heavily melodramatic.

At last the day arrived when she left the hospital, to resume her stay at Jane's. The sense of profound loneliness, of lack of all human contacts, that swept over her at this time was enough to have cowed a braver spirit.

"What's the use of trying to go straight?" she asked Jane, one day. "I've got the name—I might as well have the game."

"You talk like a fool, Honey!" Jane exclaimed.

"Do I?" Honey stared, cool, level-eyed, into her sister's face. "That's a strange remark, coming from you."

"Why from me? What do you mean?"

"Well—*you* haven't been so particular, have you? You've preached to me a lot, but what about you and Don Kendall? At least, I didn't have a husband to consider."

Jane started.

"What makes you think I ever did anything I shouldn't, as far as Don Kendall is concerned?" she asked.

"I'm not blind, Jane. I came home one night, weeks ago—that time I told you I had lost my key—and saw you in his arms."

For a moment Jane did not speak. Then she went over to Honey and placed her hand on the girl's shoulder.

"Honey dear," she said, "it's true Don kissed me that night. It's true I cared about him—or thought I did. But I give you my word of honor, that's as far as it ever went.

LOVE'S GREATEST MISTAKE 231

Don't be so depressed. Everything's going to come out all right."

But Honey shook her head and refused to be comforted.

"Why shouldn't I be depressed?" she said. "The friends I trusted have gone back on me. My brother has disowned me. The man who claimed to love me thinks I'm a hussy. I'm —done for, Jane." She began to sob. "Why, even Don, who seemed to be fond of me, has never written me even a line. And he promised he would."

"If I were you, Honey," June said, "I'd stop thinking about Don Kendall. He isn't the sort of man who can do a girl like you any good. I've been at fault, dear, filling you up with a lot of fool notions about money and all. But I'm through. When George gets home, Saturday, I'm going to have a talk with him about his company making a place for you in the New York office. I'll have him insist on it. Hard work's the thing to help a person forget trouble.

"Why don't you lie down and take a nice, long rest this afternoon? I've got to go out for a while right after lunch, but I'll be back in a couple of hours."

232   LOVE'S GREATEST MISTAKE

It was after 5 o'clock when Jane returned to the apartment. She called to Honey as she entered the hall, but received no response.

She hurried to her sister's bedroom. Honey was not there. Her suitcase was gone, her toilet articles, much of her clothing. In horror Jane stood gazing down at the empty drawers of the dressing-table. A sheet of note paper propped against the lamp caught her attention. As she saw the words written upon it her heart almost stopped beating:

Guess I won't be back, Jane [she read]. You said something about making mistakes. If I'm making one now, I'm doing it with my eyes open.   HONEY.

Jane Sommers, staring down at the empty drawers of Honey's dressing-table, read again and again the note left by her:

Guess I won't be back, Jane. You said something about making mistakes. If I'm making one now, I'm doing it with my eyes open.   HONEY.

Long-forgotten words from the Bible rose in Jane's mind: "Am I my brother's keeper?" She had been her sister's keeper, and had failed in the task. Honey was gone—to God knew what fate.

Having been held up to the world as a woman of loose morals, was it surprising that Honey refused to continue the hopeless struggle? Mr. Ogden had offered her unlimited money—had shown her, if not love, at least a deep affection. Had she turned to him in desperation, now that Herbert Gibbs, the one man who had really cared for her, had turned his back?

Jane spent an hour trying to reach Mr. Ogden by telephone. He was not at his office. Beyond that she could learn nothing.

There was Mona Terry, of course. But it seemed unlikely, after what had occurred, that Honey would have gone to her. Yet Mona might know something—might suggest something. Clutching at a straw, Jane called her up, and caught her just as she was leaving the shop.

"No," said Mona, her voice breaking a little. "I haven't seen Honey. I haven't heard from her. After all that's happened, I've been ashamed to call her up. But I'd like you to know, Jane Sommers, that, if there's anything I can do to help, you can count on me—to the last ditch. I owe that poor kid a lot—more than I like to think about. You wait for me until I get there—see? All I want is time enough to run over to my apartment and put on a clean frock. Then I'll be right up. We might as well handle this thing together."

While waiting for Mona to appear, Jane called Mr. Ogden's club. Honey had said that he lived there. After a long wait she was informed that Mr. Ogden was not in—that they could give no information as to when he would be in.

It seemed a long time before Mona arrived. Suddenly Jane was filled with new fears. Suppose Honey had decided to commit suicide! Then, with a gasping laugh, Jane remembered the empty drawers of the dressing-table—the missing mirror, brush, comb. One does not carry one's toilet articles to a rendezvous with death. The ringing of the doorbell put an end to her wild fancies.

Mona came in, bursting with energy and news. The news, however, was not of Honey, but of herself.

"I want you to know, first off," she said, "that I've gotten rid of Ray Becker. I'll tell you all about it later on. If I hadn't been crazy about him I never would have treated Honey the way I did. Have you heard anything from her yet?"

LOVE'S GREATEST MISTAKE 235

"No. I—I've been wondering, after all that's happened, if she might not have gone to—to Mr. Ogden. She's been so wretched, so unhappy, of late. I've tried to reach him at his club, but they say he isn't in."

"Of course. They would. But we'll go straight there and find out. If you've got any money with you, bring it along. We may need it before the evening is over."

A taxicab took them across the park to Fifth Avenue. Mona, more assertive than Jane, interviewed the doorman at the club.

"It is necessary," she said, regarding that functionary as if he were a worm, "for me to see Mr. William Ogden at once. A matter of life and death. If he is in the club, tell him that Mrs. Sommers has an important message for him—Mrs. Jane Sommers."

They waited interminably in the vestibule. Then, to their surprise, Mr. Ogden suddenly stood before them.

"What can I do for you?" he asked, giving his callers a curt nod.

"Honey has disappeared," Mona said bluntly. "We thought you might know something—"

"No!" Mr. Ogden showed real concern. "I

have heard nothing from her. Had anything happened to cause her to—"

"She was blue, despondent, miserable," Jane interrupted. "We thought—"

"I understand. I have always been very fond of Honey. If I hear anything of her I will let you know at once. Now, if you will excuse me—"

"*That's* out," Mona said, as they returned to the cab. "How about this man Gibbs she liked so much? Could she have gone to him?"

"I don't think so," Jane said, "but we might try."

She gave the taxi driver the number of Herbert's apartment.

The doorman was brief but explicit. Mr. Gibbs was out of town—in Chicago, on business. He had left two days before.

"Well," Jane said, when they had once more regained their cab, "there's Don Kendall, of course; but—he's in the West Indies."

Mona sat upright in her seat, almost dropping the cigarette she had just lighted.

"How do you know he isn't back?"

"I don't," said Jane.

"Then let's find out. What's his address?" Once more Jane spoke to the taxi driver.

"She'd never think of going to Don," she said.

"Why not? She loves him."

"What do you mean?"

"Just what I say. Honey's been in love with this Kendall boy from the start. Even I know that, although I only saw her with him once. That's been her whole trouble."

Jane clutched her companion's hand, shuddering.

"If she's gone to *him*," she said, "it's the end. Don never cared for a woman seriously in his life—and never will."

Mona did not answer. She was thinking of the look in Don Kendall's eyes when he had faced Ray Becker at her apartment that night and told Ray what would happen to him if he ever said anything about Honey McNeill.

CHAPTER XXVIII

Don Kendall was packing a kit bag when Honey was announced, and his surprise was so great that he asked the clerk to repeat the name a second time, to be sure he had heard aright.

"Send her—send her up," he stammered, dropping the receiver upon its hook.

Honey—of all the people in the world—coming to see him!

Yet, had thoughts of her been the only thing needed to bring her, she would long ago have been in his arms.

It was two days since he had landed from his West Indies trip—two days during which only his promise to Jane had kept him from calling Honey up; two days during which he had seen her face before him a hundred times, as he had seen it in the Canadian lakes, in the blue waters of the Gulf Stream.

Of what had happened in his absence, of the article in the newspapers, he knew nothing. His two days in New York had been spent in conferences with his father and with other officials of the company regarding the outcome of his trip. Now he was headed for Washington.

Mr. Kendall, Senior, had accomplished something he had almost despaired of accomplishing —he had interested Don in his business. The truth, had he but known it, was that Don had plunged into his new work in the hope of forgetting Honey McNeill—of driving from his mind her gay yet pathetic face.

When he drew open the door, Honey staggered in, carrying a suitcase. It was pouring outside. Dripping wet, her face dead white except for its aureole of amber-colored hair, Honey leaned against the door, staring at him. Don found his arms reaching out for her.

"Honey, darlin'," he asked uneasily, "is—is anything the matter?"

For a moment she continued to gaze at him in silence, tears coursing down her cheeks. She seemed unable to speak. Then, at length:

"Oh—Don," she whispered, "I couldn't stay away any longer. I love you. Don't you see? I love you—I can't live any longer without you! I've left my sister's. I'm never going back. I don't care what you think—what anybody thinks. I'm yours—all yours!" She swayed toward him, her hands flung out. "I'm not asking you to marry me—"

Don, staring at her amazed, saw the clear, high courage in her eyes. Then, with a laugh, he swept her, dripping as she was, into his arms.

"You—you poor kid," he whispered. "Come in here and take those wet things off before you get pneumonia. Then we'll have a talk."

He put his arms around her—almost pushed her into the bedroom.

"Strip," he commanded. "There's a bathrobe in the closet. Throw your clothes through the door and I'll have them dried in no time. Then come out here and I'll fix you a hot drink."

To the valet who presently answered his summons he handed Honey's soaked dress, her lingerie, her stockings and shoes, without a smile. Nor did the valet smile. Young Mr. Kendall was too important, too self-willed a person, to be criticized.

He returned as Honey flapped into the room. The bathrobe in which she was enveloped hung in great wings over her arms, trailed like a robe of state upon the floor. Don turned back the cuffs, tucked her away among soft pillows in a corner of the couch, gave her the hot drink he had promised. Then he stood upon the hearthrug, gazing at her quizzically.

"Now, youngster," he said at length, "tell me what it's all about."

"Why—why—" Honey's tragedies seemed to have vanished, now that she was with him once more. "Everyone's been so horrid to me—has believed such terrible things about me—that I—I couldn't stand it. So I came to you."

"How did you know I was back?"

"I telephoned."

"Then you don't think I—believe terrible things about you?"

"Do you, Don?"

He laughed, a deep, full laugh, at this.

"You silly kid. Haven't I known, ever since that first night I kissed you, just the sort of girl you are? Do you suppose anybody could make me think different? Good Lord, Honey—I'm not a fool! I know you're—all right. That's why I've kept away from you. One reason."

"Was there another one?"

"Yes. I told you about it before. Your sister thought I—I'd gobble you up. Like a wolf or something."

"And was it because of Jane you didn't write?"

"Yes; I promised I wouldn't."

Honey gazed reflectively at her small pink toes.

"Well," she asked, "now that I'm here, what are you going to do with me?"

All the visions that Don had seen in crystal lakes, in shimmering skies, in green-and-gold stretches of sea, merged into delicious reality. "I'm going to take you to Washington with me," he said. "But I've got a couple of business matters to attend to downtown first. Thomas will have your things back, all pressed and everything, in a little while, so you might as well drive down with me. In fact, I think I hear him coming now. Which gives us just time for that kiss I've been longing for ever since you came in here. I love you, Honey child. You—you're my sweetheart—my darling."

She was in his arms now, sobbing against his breast, kissing him hungrily, rapturously, through her tears, rejoicing at the passion that had suddenly made them one.

"I've wanted you so—wanted you so!" she whispered, her heart singing with joy.

LOVE'S GREATEST MISTAKE

Then the valet knocked loudly on the door.

The suite in the big hotel in Washington was charming, with its cozy parlor, its bedroom and bath adjoining. Honey smiled for an instant as she glanced at the twin beds, then looked at her watch. Half-past twelve. What could be keeping Don, she wondered. He had left her, gone downstairs immediately upon their arrival a short time before.

She felt suddenly lonely, here in this strange place. Suppose he did not come back? Suppose he should never come back? The thought so terrified her for a moment, that she gripped the edge of the dresser for support. Then she began to undress.

Did Don really love her? Or had he acted on the impulse of the moment? As she had. If only she could be sure!

She loved him. She thought that love was scarcely an adequate word. She adored him. She could have kissed the floor where he had walked upon it. Madness, she thought—and was proud that she felt as she did.

He had been wonderful during the long ride on the train. Dinner had been a thing of joyous laughter—at trifles, because they were both a little nervous, unstrung.

She took off the crêpe frock she wore, and hung it carefully in the closet along with her slip. It seemed immodest, somehow, to leave her intimate garments lying around where Don could see them. Wearing only a filmy step-in, she sat on the edge of the bed and slowly took off her shoes and stockings.

These, too, she put out of sight, and, opening her suitcase, drew from it a silk nightdress, very delicate and sheer. It was a new one that she had bought, along with some other articles, in the afternoon, after leaving her sister's apartment.

It had taken high courage to go to Don, to offer herself to him without conditions of any sort, just because she loved him. She had spent two hours in the shops, revolving the matter in her mind, trying to arrive at a decision. It was not until she had reached it that she bought the silk nightdress. A symbol of freedom, she had thought it then—a banner of love, gayly pink and fluttering.

She threw it across the foot of one of the twin beds, and, going into the bathroom, turned on the water in the shiny porcelain tub.

While waiting for it to fill she arranged her toilet articles—toothbrush, paste, powder, perfume, other little things—on the shelves of the medicine closet.

Already, she thought with a queer smile, she was beginning to make herself at home. After all, homes were just places in which one arranged one's belongings. A suitcase—a vanload—no great difference. A home with—friends—children?

The tub was full now. She slipped out of the step-in and into the warm water.

It felt very fresh and pleasant, perfumed by the tablets and the bath soap she had bought that afternoon. When she finally stepped from the tub to dry herself, she suggested a young and somewhat timid wood nymph emerging from her forest pool, glancing around as if fearful of prying eyes among the bushes.

The bedroom, with its single rose-shaded reading-lamp, invited her. Honey's joyousness, for a time dulled, came back to her. She was breathless at the thought of Don's return, of the great adventure of love on which she was embarked.

As she drew the thin silk nightdress over her head she was trembling as if with a chill. Had he come back, she wondered. A wisp of cigarette smoke, curling between the drawn curtains at the sitting-room door, answered her question.

The knowledge of his nearness both thrilled and frightened her. She could hear him walking around—knew from the sounds that came to her that he was undressing.

For a moment she felt a desire to run away. Then she heard the faint sound of footsteps, as Don, in his bare feet, walked nervously up and down the room, waiting for her to call him.

With a laugh that was very close to a sob, Honey drew back the counterpane and sheet of the bed farthest from the door. Then she crept beneath the covers and drew them protectingly over her. Reaching out one bare arm, she switched off the shaded reading-lamp at her side.

The room was in darkness now, except for the faint threads of light around the edges of the curtained doorway. The sound of footsteps in the adjoining parlor ceased. Honey suddenly found her throat very hot and dry, her whole body shaking. Beneath every other thought, every other emotion, lay the hope that Don really believed in her—knew her to be a decent woman.

"Don," she called, in a little voice. It was

a call that came from the depths of her heart.

The clatter of metal told her that the curtains were being thrust aside. She heard the brass rings slide swiftly along the rod. Almost before she realized it, she lay in his arms.

It was difficult to speak, with her lips pressed so tightly against his, but she managed it.

"Dearest," she whispered, "you know, don't you, that there has never been—any other man —but—but you?"

He seemed scarcely to listen to her. She heard him laughing joyously.

"Why don't you answer me?" she whispered.

"Isn't the fact that I'm laughing at you answer enough?" he said. "You're *mine!*"

Honey was awakened by the ringing of the telephone bell. As she took up the receiver she saw that the bed beside hers was empty.

"Mrs. Kendall," a man's voice came to her, "your sister, Mrs. Sommers, is calling. And Miss Terry. Shall I send them up?"

For an instant Honey hesitated, speechless. Jane—Mona—downstairs! It was incredible.

"Shall I send them up?" the voice repeated.
"Yes."

There was nothing else to do. Don would

get rid of them, Honey thought. She supposed him to be in the next room, dressing. Snatching up a negligée, she ran into the parlor.

Don, however, was not there. The absence of his clothes showed that he had gone out. Honey flew back into the bedroom, glanced at her watch. It was 10 o'clock. Amazed that she had slept so long, she went to the dressing-table. There was a sheet of paper propped against the mirror. On it was written:

Hadn't the heart to wake you up, darling—you looked so comfy. Back soon. Love.   Don.

Honey snatched up the bit of paper and kissed it.

When Jane came in, followed by Mona Terry, she could scarcely keep from laughing, their faces were so tragic.

"What can you be thinking of?" Jane demanded, staring angrily at her sister.

"Right now," Honey answered, "I'm wondering what brought you two here."

"Wait a moment," Mona interrupted. "We've been dreadfully worried about you, Honey. Ever since yesterday afternoon. First we went to Mr. Ogden. Then we tried Mr. Gibbs. Neither of them knew anything about you. At Mr. Kendall's apartment we learned that he had left for Washington with—with a girl. We decided it must be you, so we came down by sleeper."

"What for?" Honey asked.

"Why, to—to save you from doing something you'd regret. None of my business, I suppose, but— To tell you the truth, Honey, I've had you on my conscience—"

"You've got to leave this—this man," Jane said, "and come back to New York with me at once. I can't let you disgrace the family."

Honey began to laugh.

"Disgrace the family!" she exclaimed, sitting on the arm of a chair. "Haven't I done that already? Or, rather, haven't the newspapers done it for me? Didn't dear brother Martin say in his letter that he was 'through with me'—that I was never to 'darken his door' again?"

Jane was crying now, the tears running down her cheeks.

"To think that any man could do such a thing to—to my sister!" she sobbed. "Tempt her from home—"

"Oh, piffle!" Honey laughed. "If there was any tempting, I did it. Right now I'm too happy to think of such disagreeable things. When Don gets here—"

He came in just then, smiling joyously. Even the presence of these unexpected guests did not dull his look of happiness.

Honey sprang up—ran to his arms.

"They think I've done something terrible, Don, dear!" she cried.

"Do they?" There was a ripple of laughter in Don Kendall's big voice.

Jane stared at him, her eyes dark with anger.

"I don't know whether you realize it or not, Mr. Kendall," she said, "but Honey is a good girl—or was when she left my apartment yesterday. Whatever you may have thought about her and Mr. Ogden was wrong. The whole affair was just a rotten frame-up. Miss Terry knows the truth about it. She's come all the way from New York to tell you."

"I don't need Miss Terry, or you, or anyone else to tell me that Honey is a good girl," Don said sternly. "I know it without being told."

He turned to Honey, who was staring at him in adoration. "Haven't you explained things to them, sweetness?"

"No," Honey grinned. "They seemed so tragic, I hadn't the heart to undeceive them."

LOVE'S GREATEST MISTAKE 251

Don drew a folded document from his pocket.

"Look here, you two," he said. "Honey and I were married late yesterday afternoon, before we left New York. Got the license just as the bureau was closing. If you'd like to see our marriage certificate, here it is." He extended the paper to Jane. "Stick around for a while, why don't you, and we'll order up the well-known wedding breakfast."

Mona Terry fell into a chair.

"Well," she laughed, "ain't life a gamble? Here I had Honey all figured out as making love's greatest mistake, and she cops the solid gold wedding ring."

"I think," Honey said, her arm through Don's, "that love's greatest mistake is lack of courage. Suppose I hadn't gone to Don and told him how I felt about him!"

"I wouldn't advise most girls to take such a chance," Jane remarked.

"Neither would I," Honey agreed. "They'd never find a man like Don."

"That's what they all say," Miss Terry observed cynically.

But, as she spoke under her breath, the others did not hear her.

THE END